Vowel Play
Cliff Robison

Rock and Fire Press
Salinas, CA

Vowel Play
© 2021 by Cliff Robison

Library of Congress Catalog Number:

ISBN-13:
978-1-949005-18-9 (print)
978-1-949005-19-6 (eBook)
FIRST EDITION
First Printing

Rock and Fire Press
Salinas, CA

DISCLAIMER:

This is a work of fiction.
All of the persons and events described, and most of the places,
are figments of the author's imagination. Any resemblance
to real persons and real events is purely coincidental.

N*I*A*C*IN denies any involvement.

Chapter One

"SO, ABOUT YOUR NAME."

He gave her the expressionless face that he gave everyone. "You might as well get it over with," he said.

"O, like O. Henry? O'Callahan? Oscar, Oliver? Omega Man?"

"Just plain O. The fifteenth letter of the alphabet. It's not an initial. Doesn't stand for anything. Just a nickname."

"What's your real name?"

He continued the expressionless stare. He was expecting this; he had gone through it thousands of times. He took a moment to size her up, weighing whether he really wanted to tell her his name.

She seemed friendly enough, he supposed, and he figured that she really wasn't trying to aggravate him. She was naturally curious. She had to be, to have a gig like this.

"Imagine this," he said, after a long pause. "You're the night nurse in a maternity ward in a small Idaho town. One night, there's a couple who come in just as she's about to give birth. The man is huge – not just tall, but muscled to fit. The woman gets woozy when the doctor gives her the epidural. By the time the baby arrives, she's on another planet.

"You fill out the paperwork with the information the man gives you, but you stop at the baby's name. You try to figure out a polite way not to sound condescending, when you ask if that's really what he wants you to write down. So you ask if the mother would want that for the baby's name. He gives you a look that makes you think twice.

"You write down the baby's name, because it can always be changed later, if the mother disagrees. Besides, you never want to see that man give you that look ever again."

"I'm intrigued," she said. "And what was the name?"

"Vowel."

She opened her mouth, realized what he said, and closed her mouth. "Your father named you Vowel?" she asked, eyes wide.

"Vowel Johnson. Known to my friends as O." His voice was flat, and he could have been describing the weather forecast. "Now, how does this work?"

"Ah, well, you've passed the background check," she said. "And I have to tell you that if you're involved, even slightly, in one of our cases, you have to take a leave of absence until it's over."

"Not from around here," he said. "Which is why I'm here."

"Me neither," she said. "Ashland, down by California." She slid a paper across the table to him. "Initial that I just told you about the conflicts clause."

He wrote the letters OJ. She thought of making him put VJ, but she decided not to push it.

"So, we can't investigate any active case. Initial that." He did so. "And we can't take on any case unless the Sheriff specifically gives it to us." He initialed the next line. "We don't get paid. We do this as a hobby." Another OJ.

She looked up at him and frowned. "You're very young to be retired," she said.

"I'm not." He looked back down at the form, but she wasn't going on until he explained. "I'm on a leave of absence from a job at a bank in Dunsmuir."

"Medical?"

He sighed softly. "No. I killed three people at work. So they don't want me back at work. But I wasn't charged with a crime, so they can't fire me."

"Did you tell the sheriff that in your interview?"

"Of course."

"And he still passed your background check?"

"It was justifiable. California Penal Code section 189. It was me or them. Plus, I saved all of my coworkers. Those guys killed everybody at the last two banks they robbed." He shrugged. "So what do you do with a guy who can't be fired but can't come back to work either?"

"I guess you pester him till he moves an entire state away."

"And that's how I came to be applying for this gig. I need something useful to do with my time."

"So, do you have any law enforcement background?"

"None."

"Military?"

"None. Is this on the form?"

"No, we're done with the paperwork. I was just curious how you came to join the auxiliary. It's usually wives or widows of policemen, once in a while a mystery buff. Althea Malpaso, who originally founded the auxiliary, she was a real mystery buff. Thought she was the reincarnation of Old Harriet Vane."

"I have no idea who that is."

"A mystery character. Tea cozy crime stories. Dorothy L. Sayers used to write about her."

"Ah." O was saved from explaining his abhorrence of crime fiction by the timely appearance of Sheriff Langer. Langer's uniform, as always, was crisp and pressed, as though it had just come from the dry cleaner. Sharp creases ran down along the centers of each short pocket. His mustache had been precisely trimmed, stopping exactly one millimeter above the vermilion border of his upper lip, and ending on each side a precise two millimeters from the corners of his mouth.

"O, I see you've met Millicent," he said. "When you're done here, would you stop in my office?"

"Surely," said O, rising from his chair a few inches as he shook Langer's hand.

Langer continued on his way, leaving the two sitting at the small wooden table in a break room that barely contained it.

"You know the sheriff," said Millicent.

"Vaguely. We met a long time ago."

"Is that what qualifies you? Knowing the sheriff?"

O did not immediately answer. He instead slowly scanned Millicent Milford, taking in the hair – salt and pepper, with an emphasis on salt; closely cropped in a haircut that would have seemed excessively short on a middle-aged man. She wore a shapeless flannel shirt two sizes too large, open down the front, as a jacket over a black T-shirt with no logos.

"You said that most folks in the auxiliary are wives, widows, and mystery buffs," he said. "Which are you?"

"None of the above. I have two talents. First, I don't trust the police. And second, I know a lot of people. The latter makes me useful for solving cold cases, because I hear a lot of gossip, and the former makes me useful for keeping power in check."

O had to concede that she was very forthright. It remained to be seen if her self-analysis was accurate or even justified. He decided to be as frank with her.

"I have an IQ of 183," he said. "I once scored a 187 on a test, and conventional wisdom is to take the highest score, but I suspect that the proctor in that test was a bit sloppy in his calculations. I try not to tell people my IQ, because they often either fear me or despise me because of it. If I had a nickel for every time I've been told that I think I'm *so smart* ..." He shrugged.

Millicent raised an eyebrow in reassessment.

"How are you at Trivial Pursuits?"

"It's hard to say. No one will play me more than once."

Millicent nodded. "My nieces and nephews won't even play Monopoly with me. And Scrabble is right out."

"You have no children of your own?"

She guffawed. "No," she said, when she had composed her face. "None at all." She gathered the pages he had initialed and placed them back onto the clipboard. "We should have an ID for you in a couple weeks," she said. "Do not use it to tell people that you're a cop. It's not a get out of jail free card. And it won't prevent a parking ticket."

O nodded.

Millie waved her hand, dismissing him.

"Millie Millie is a misanthrope," said Langer.

O looked at him blankly for a moment, to satisfy himself that Langer wasn't quoting a nursery rhyme of some sort. Then he slowly nodded.

6

"My first thought on meeting her was that she didn't like men. It's not that at all. She doesn't like mankind. Humans," said Langer.

"That seems a bit harsh. She seemed friendly enough."

"Wait till you get to know her. She smiles and smiles. I'm told that she's very active in a variety of clubs. But…" he shrugged.

"Cat lady?"

"Doubt she'd appreciate them. No, I'm thinking one extreme or the other. Goldfish or Tasmanian devils."

"Ah," said O. It was one of his casual placeholder remarks. He used it to signal that he understood and had nothing to say in response. He sometimes varied it with "There you go" or perhaps "Nice day for it."

"Reason I called you in here… Know anything about wine?"

It was clearly a rhetorical question, so O merely raised a single eyebrow in response.

Langer continued. "Does it turn into vinegar?"

"It can, if the cork dries out. Depends on the type of wine, how much air gets into the bottle, things like that."

"Properly sealed, neck turned down, rotated weekly to prevent sediment from collecting. All the proper procedures, done by professionals who know their stuff."

"No. Not unless it was vinegar when it was bottled."

Langer frowned. "That's what I thought. Thanks, O."

O rose at the obvious dismissal, and left without a word.

Chapter Two

"SO, THE MCNULTY CASE." said Millie. She opened a folder in front of O. "1978. Two people were murdered; there was no obvious motive, and no obvious connection.

"The man was plumbing contractor. Investigators initially believed he was there about a leaking water heater. He had a wrench in his hand, and he fell into a small puddle. Slightly loose fitting for the water heater relief valve. Shot once in the chest, once in the head. Fell down the steps into the basement.

"The woman was in the kitchen cooking breakfast for one. Not for herself; coroner said that she had already eaten. Three eggs over hard. By the time police arrived, they were burning, and set off the smoke alarm. That's what triggered discovery of the bodies."

"How was the woman dressed?"

"Blouse, slacks, flat shoes, but nice ones."

"Husband did it."

"Aren't you jumping to a conclusion? He was down in Eugene to give a series of lectures on mine safety."

"No, he wasn't."

"Explain."

"Contractor and wife were having an affair. Husband knew it and arranged an alibi. She wouldn't be cooking in the clothes she intended to wear to work. Too much chance of ruining her good

8

clothes. Also, no one cooks three eggs over hard. It would be two over hard, or two and one over easy, or two and two.

"Husband arranges a time gap in Eugene, sneaks out, drives home. Loosens the relief valve on the water heater. He could do that by hand, with no tools. He probably also ran out all the hot water, so that the wife would have to call the contractor.

"He hides until she calls the contractor. He shoots the wife. Contractor, who is looking at the water heater because his lover asked him to, comes running up the stairs. He gets one in the chest, rolls down the stairs, and probably gets a second shot for insurance.

"The husband puts bread into the toaster and cracks a couple eggs into the skillet. All done."

She sighed. "Yeah, that's about right. He confessed when the stolen items were found in the trunk of his car. Revenge made to look like a burglary gone wrong." She picked up the folder. "Try this one."

She put a new folder in front of him: A series of smash and grab robberies of Jewelry stores in the northern part of the county. Different shops, different owners. All the events had occurred at around 4 AM, local time.

"Solved quickly, I hope," said O.

"Took six months and a long series of secret stakeouts. Even setting up a sting jewelry shop didn't work."

"Of course not. It wasn't a series of smash and grabs. It was insurance fraud."

Millie raised an eyebrow.

"No jeweler leaves real jewelry in his shop window at night. The real stuff goes into the safe at closing, and costume jewelry goes into the display window."

Millie frowned.

"The critical question is whether there was an owner in common among all the shops."

Millie shook her head.

"Then it was a conspiracy," said O. "A conspiracy of jewelers to defraud the insurance companies that covered the stores. The real jewelry would have been sold months before and replaced with paste replicas. At the appointed hour, the window is shattered, the paste is stolen, and the insurance picks up the pieces."

"And the costume jewelry?"

"Toxic. Smartest thing would be to ship it to China without a return address. Next best choice would be to sink it in the river." He sipped the coffee in the tiny styrofoam cup. He couldn't decide if he liked it or not. It didn't have the rich Arabica flavor that Washington was known for, but it wasn't bad, for Robusta.

"We found shipping labels addressed to Guangdong province in the shops of one of the jewelers," Millie sighed. "So did you look up these cases before coming in?"

"No," said O. He sipped the coffee again. It would do, he decided. As something to lift the fog and to get the gears turning, it would serve. "It just seems to me that that's how they would work."

"Okay, that makes you four for four on old cases. I guess you really are qualified to be on the team."

"Are there really any actual qualifications?" O asked. "I got the idea that it was kind of an *ad hoc* hobby sort of a thing. Anybody with ideas, so to speak." He shrugged.

"Well," she said, "It's nice when everyone brings something to the table, you understand."

"I've never understood that metaphor," said O. "What sort of a table are we talking about? A bargaining table? A dinner table? A card table? Are we imagining that solving crimes is like a potluck dinner? If we take a scoop of my memories and a spoonful of your contacts, we'll suddenly have the solution?

"Or is it supposed to be some sort of negotiation? I'll contribute my skills if you back my theory of the crime, and next week I'll back your theory: is that how it works?"

Millie colored slightly and pursed her lips.

"I suppose you prefer working alone," she said.

"It's not that I prefer it," he said, calmly stating the simple fact. "But it is often the smoothest."

Millie got up and walked out, leaving him to wonder, as he often did, whether he had offended her, and if so, how.

A largish woman in a flowery muumuu swept into the room. She glided to the coffeemaker, poured herself a cup, and then spun around with an unexpected grace, to look O in the eye.

"You must be O," she said. "They call me triple-A." She smiled. "Sheriff Langer said that you're old friends."

He wondered at the reason for such a nickname. He assumed that she would not use it in self-reference if it pertained to a tow truck, so the obvious answer was out.

"Triple-A," he said. "Well, it's nice to meet you."

"My initials," she explained, holding out an overly-ringed hand. He wondered how she could use the hand without the rings interfering with her movement. Each finger had at least one, including the thumb.

When he offered his own hand, she pinched his fingers between her fingertips for the briefest of moments. "I also go by Ann. It's my middle name. But it's nice to know I'm not the only person in this world whose parents had an odd sense of humor."

"In my experience, it seems to be a common failing among parents. Creative names, that is."

"Well, I suppose that my last name made it inevitable. It must have been irresistible for them. Abeddyon."

O thought for a moment. "Tell me that your first name isn't something like Aiden."

Triple-A sighed. "I wish I could, but I can't. Just call me Ann." She cocked her head towards the door. "Don't worry about Millie-Millie. She'll get used to you in time. She hates everyone."

The muumuu glided out of the break room towards a tiny room packed full of communications equipment. "Sheriff's Call Center," he heard her say, as she arranged herself in front of the console. "What is the nature of your emergency?"

The Pacific County Volunteer Citizen Review Board, or the Cold Case Think Tank, as it was more commonly called, met weekly at the very least, excepting holidays and special events. O spent the next six days drinking coffee and working jigsaw puzzles.

Thursday afternoon, O arrived early. He brought a small box of doughnuts, a baker's dozen assortment. He started to put it on the small counter next to the coffee machine, but then decided to center it on the table. And that led to a dilemma: Should he take a doughnut, allowing everyone to think he had brought fewer doughnuts, or should he wait until the others arrived?

He decided to content himself with coffee for the time being, and began perusing the bulletin board. Police League Activities for Youth was holding a tee-ball signup and bake sale. Someone on the graveyard shift – the third watch – was selling a mountain bike. Someone was having some sort of meeting. Someone was selling silicone bakeware.

He forced himself to read each item a second time, not out of any interest, but simply to occupy the time.

Millie was the second to arrive. She glanced at the box. "Trying to make us all fat?" she asked. "Shelley Colfax won't be here. She's trying to finish her knitting."

"How many others are coming?"

"You and me and the cat makes three," said Millie.

Triple-A swept into the room on a beeline for the coffee machine. She came about suddenly and glanced at the box. "O, that is so sweet," she said. "Sheriff Langer never brings doughnuts."

She helped herself to a chocolate cake doughnut with sprinkles, waving her ring-encrusted fingers at them as she glided out of the room.

"As if she needs doughnuts," said Millie.

"Well, there's the cat, so I guess we're all here," said O. He took a jelly-filled and sat down at the table.

Millie frowned. She took a seat, ignored the doughnuts, and flipped open a well-worn spiral notebook to a page in the middle. "Minutes of the last meeting," she started to say.

"I'm willing to dispense with the reading of the minutes," he said. "Since you're the only person here who can verify them, I propose that we let them stand as written, and move on to old business."

She furrowed her brow and pursed her mouth for a moment.

"The Pennington Case is concluded," she said, reading from her notebook. "On the recommendation of this committee, the investigators re-examined the door latch and found that the kitchen door lock had been picked open. This led to the confession of John Symmons of Long Beach."

There was a moment of silence.

"There is no further old business on the floor," she said.

"I suppose new business is up next?"

"Well, if Shelley were here, I'd formally introduce you to the group, but since we're dispensing with niceties today, we'll skip it."

"So noted," he said. Millie wondered if he thought he was running the meeting, or if he was just mocking her parliamentary procedures. She might need to have a little talk with O, just to set the proper boundaries.

"And the floor is now open for discussion," she said.

"I suppose that the pertinent question is whether we have any new cases to work on. Or would that be under 'New business?' "

Millie shook her head, and as she did, the door opened. Sheriff Langer stepped in. "Millie," he asked, "You know anything at all about wine?"

"People drink it," she said.

Langer grimaced. "You two feel up for a small road trip?" He spotted the box of doughnuts and flipped the box open with his finger. A glazed old-fashioned caught his eye.

"How far?" said Millie.

"About forty minutes each way," he said. "Need some eyes on something down by Ilwaco."

"I'd better not be late for my bridge night," muttered Millie.

"I'm up for it," said O.

"Go to the Ilwaco Pool and Poker Club, #21 Highway 100. Meet with a Jackson Johns. Tell him you're working with the sheriff's department. Remember to say, 'With.' Do not, and I will repeat, do *not* identify yourselves as sheriff's deputies or sheriff's detectives. Are we clear?"

"Absolutely," said Millie.

"Sure," said O.

The car they drew from the county carpool was an ancient Chrysler Coronet two-door. It had once been olive green, and was the paint was unevenly oxidized, though no actual rust showed through. A car collector would say that it had its "original patina." There were ridges in the paint on the doors, where a police emblem had been scraped off and replaced with a Pacific County logo. A metal bar, now devoid of lights, stretched over the roof just behind the front doors.

Inside, the upholstery had been refurbished, but not recently, and shoulder straps had been added to bring the car up to current state safety requirements. Two obvious holes in the dashboard upholstery showed where the radio mount had been summarily ripped out. The cigarette lighter was missing, and whether this was a nod to the county's non-smoking policy, or merely a victim of time and entropy, O couldn't begin to guess.

O glanced at the odometer. It claimed 59,483 miles. O wondered if it had flipped twice, for over a quarter-million miles, or only once. Not that it mattered. So long as county maintenance certified it as roadworthy, it would do.

Millie picked up a clipboard from the transmission hump and wrote down, in the designated columns, that the PCVCRB were taking the car, and that the starting mileage was 59,483. She wrote OJ for the driver and MM in the notes column.

"Do we fill that out any time we use a county car?" he asked.

"It's a requirement. Unauthorized use is a criminal offense."

"The notes column; is that where we keep track of out-of-state plates we've seen? Two Montana plates already. Well done."

She gave him an icy stare. He ignored it and started the engine.

The Ilwaco Pool and Poker Club was a roadside shack made of untreated lumber. Parts of the side appeared to be a batten board style, others shiplap. All of the wood had turned gray with age, and some of the boards had deep grooves, where rainwater had washed away the cellulose, leaving mainly just lignin.

The shack was at the edge of the Cape Disappointment State Park, near the old Cape Disappointment lighthouse. In the light mist that sifted down through the air, it seemed dark and dismal, though an inviting yellow light gleamed from a single lightly frosted window near the back.

O turned into a parking lot, consisting of an oval-shaped patch of gravel, punctuated at the edges and corners by dandelions and thin stalks of tall grasses and weeds. A small white patch of slush, a memorial to the last snowfall, nestled against one of the north-facing walls. O parked with the rear wheels on the gravel, in case it rained while they were inside.

Darkness, like a bear cave in the dead of winter, seemed to be the décor inside the pool hall. The window that had offered the inviting yellow light was not either of the heavily-tinted windows that O could see from inside the club. A string of tiny Christmas lights, mostly yellow, ran along the ceiling just where it met the walls. Some of the segments were dark, creating gaps in the line.

Only the tiny lights around the ceiling and the muffled sunlight filtering past the darkened windows offered any light at all.

As O's eyes adjusted, he became aware of a pool table at one end of the room, and a snooker table at the other. Neither was in play, and O had the vague impression that the pool table had one low corner. All of the balls were at one side, bracing against a cue stick that had been flung haphazardly across the felt.

In the middle of the room, there were a handful of single-leg tables, each with peeling formica veneer over plywood, balanced on shiny chrome shafts with scratched-up chrome bases. A nervous-looking man sat by himself, at a table that pressed against the wall. He was sipping from a wineglass that held something clear. Aside from the one man, the room looked deserted.

O approached him with caution. Millie followed.

"Jackson Johns?" asked O.

"One and the same," said Johns. He turned a glassy eye towards Millie. "Ma'am," he said. "You must be the folks from Sheriff Langer's office."

Millie took the other seat, and O seated himself. Johns, however, rose unsteadily to his feet. "Anything I can get you?" he asked, bowing slightly to the pair.

"Are you the bartender?" asked Millie.

"Nope," said Johns. "It's a co-op, sort of. Pay for what you drink; drink what you pay for." He looked at O.

"Water," said O. "Or coffee if you have it."

"What's that you're drinking?" asked Millie.

"Wine," said Johns. "Our house white, you see. From a box. A cardboard box. But I sniffed the flap, and it seems that it was a very good week. Best we have, I'm afraid."

"A glass of red, then," she said. Johns, true to his word, drew a glass of red wine for her, from a box in a refrigerator. There was the sound of a microwave, and moments later Johns returned to the table, carrying a mug of coffee for O, and Millie's wine in a stem glass that didn't match his own.

"Instant," he said, gesturing to the coffee. "But caffeinated. Cream and sugar are on the bar." He dropped back into his seat and gave them both a slightly vacant look.

"You called the sheriff's department about something to do with wine," said O.

Johns put his finger across his lip and turned from side to side in an exaggerated survey of the room. They were manifestly alone, but Johns leaned close to prevent eavesdroppers.

"Got some Xino Chymo in from Greece last month. Very special ouzu, very rare. Five grand or more a bottle, retail. We get it wholesale for thirty-five hundred. Bought twenty bottles. Sold thirty. And there are five in inventory."

"Splits," asked O, "Or did some of them get returned?"

"Full bottles. Every one of 'em consumed at a dinner service." He leaned back a little. "Pair nicely with Patagonian Toothfish."

"So where did the other ten bottles come from?"

"Good question," said Johns. "Got some Arizona Trocken Wieder Gobi, out of Casa Grande. Twenty-four bottles they sent on speculation. Wholesales at six bucks even. Tried one. It was like liquid sawdust, it was so dry. The tannins could have been used to make dinosaur leather. Have not sold a single bottle. But out of twenty-three left in that case, there's only thirteen now."

"You think someone is re-labeling bad wines as good?" asked O. He sipped his coffee, then added a packet of sugar in the hopes of overcoming the freezer-burned flavor.

"Nope," said Johns. "I think they're re-bottling 'em." He leaned back all the way, drank a slug of his boxed white wine, and smiled. Probably because he was glad it wasn't Trocken Wieder Gobi, O supposed.

"Wash out an empty Xino, pour in a Trocken," said O. "Cork it, seal it... How is Xino normally sealed?"

"Foil overwrap," said Johns. "We do it ourselves when we split down another wine."

"Split?" asked Millie. "How do you split a wine?"

"Say someone doesn't want an entire bottle," said O. "You pour off half into another bottle. Or into a carafe. Customer gets the carafe, and you re-cork the half that's left. Next person to ask for a split gets the other half."

"Is it okay to do that?"

Johns shrugged. "Not really. It decants the wine – too much air in the bottle. So you need to sell the other half of the split within about two weeks. We never split an expensive wine, or one that no one ever orders."

"Alright," said O. "So we're looking at a continuing criminal enterprise to commit grand larceny."

"Conspiracy," said Millie. She looked askance at O. They shouldn't be investigating an active case. What was this new guy thinking? Who did he think he was?

"Call it whatever you like," said Johns, with an almost imperceptible slurring of his words. "It stinks. And it's not the only thing that isn't right over there at the hotel. In six or seven months, a new management company is taking over. Big professional firm out of Chicago. There's gonna be a reckoning. And I don't wanna be the guy holding the bottle." He chuckled a little at his own joke.

"Holding the bag," corrected Millie.

"Tomato, Potato," said Johns.

"Do you have any evidence of wrongdoing?" asked O.

"Aside from we're selling more wine than we bought? Aside from invoices and sales receipts?" Johns turned around and picked up a folder from the table behind him, handing it to O. "And they all got my name on them. Plus, there's this."

O hadn't noticed the wine bottle on the floor by Johns' feet until Johns plunked it in the middle of the table. He stared at it. Meerwasser Blaues. The name meant nothing to O. He showed the cobalt bottle to Millie.

"Wow," she said. "That stuff's not cheap."

"If it were Meerwasser Blaues, 1936, it would be worth about thirteen thousand dollars. Maybe more at auction, or to a collector. But turn it upside down."

O turned the bottle neck-down, and was promptly rewarded with a stream of miniscule droplets that dripped onto the table. He touched one and held it to his nose, sniffed, and then carefully touched it to his tongue.

"Vinegar," he said.

"Meerwasser Vineyards uses a compressed cork and tapered bottleneck. You can't pull the cork; it swells into a tapered shape. You can only press it down, into the bottle, using a special rabbit."

Millie raised her eyebrows. "A rabbit?" She imagined a cartoon with magician's pets in top hats, trained to serve wine.

"It's a device used to open wine bottles," said O. "It looks vaguely like a rabbit's head, and pulling the ears will lever the cork out of the neck."

"Except here," said Johns. "With this bottle, the rabbit pushes the cork down, into the bottle. But then, of course, you can't recork the bottle –"

"Because a cork floating in the wine will be a dead giveaway that it was tampered with."

"Give that man a cigar," said Johns. "So they used a hypodermic needle. A big one."

"Probably a trocar," said O. "It's a huge needle used to extract fluids in medical procedures."

"Yeah, sure," said Johns. "Anyway, it damaged the cork. You can see little crumbs of cork floating down there in the wine – in the vinegar. So air gets in, and the cheap wine they used to replace the expensive wine gets oxidized."

"What about the Meerwasser?" asked Millie.

"Probably sold it in carafes. Or two carafes, as a split. Each table thinks the other got the bottle, but it's still the Meerwasser. And people who know Meerwasser will recognize the taste."

"A bit salty?" asked O.

"No, not at all," said Johns, his brow furrowing. "Slightly fruity, excellent legs, nice bouquet, mild hints of apple and lemon, pepper back, and an exceptionally smooth finish."

"So the bottle with the cheap wine – if this hadn't turned to vinegar, it would have been sold – ?"

"To someone who didn't know Meerwasser. And it would have been an insult to the Meerwasser name, and the diner would likely never order Meerwasser ever again. Why would they, when they can get the same dreck for five dollars at any liquor store? Or better? Heck, they might even sell this stuff in hardware stores."

"So long term, it's pointless, but short term, it's a nice fiddle."

"Sorry," said Millie, "But why is it pointless?"

"Because you sting your customers once, and make lots of money short-term, but customers stop buying your expensive wines, so you lose money long term," recapped O.

"Not to mention that eventually the vineyard gets complaints and calls you to find out what exactly you're selling under their trademarked label," confirmed Johns.

"And if it's badly-repackaged vinegar," finished O, "You've got some explaining to do. So who do you think is behind this?"

Johns looked around the little room, even though the three of them were the only souls in the place. "All of them," he whispered.

Chapter Three

LUNCH WAS DELICIOUS. AS Johns' guests, they ate at a little café on the ground floor. Well, ground floor was a misnomer: From the parking circle, it was on the ground floor. From the other side of the building, it overlooked a steep cliff and the rocks far below, where the waves crashed against the cliff before being swept back by the river. To the left, a stand of small pines marked the beginning of the herb garden, behind the kitchen.

"If anyone asks, you're my cousins from California," said Johns, in an undertone. He pointed to the glass in front of Millie. "Swirl it. See how there's a transparent residue that takes a moment to rejoin the rest? That tells you how sweet or how dry it is."

"I've never heard a wine called 'sweet,' " said O.

"We usually say 'fruity' or something like that. If you get strong fruit flavor, it's a sweet wine; if there is a tannin flavor along the sides of your tongue, that's a dry wine. In between, you might say that a wine tastes 'nutty' or that it has subtle overtones of acidity. Something like that."

"Code words," said Millie, stiffening her spine. "Elitist dog whistles." Johns just shrugged in reply.

O stirred his coffee, blending the cream and sugar into the dark mix. When he sipped it, there was no acidity that he could taste, though there was just enough sweetness to counteract the native bitterness of the beans. The cream gave it body. The sides of his tongue told him that the coffee was hot. Regarding tannins, his palate was silent. And the coffee had no aftertaste, so he supposed that it could be said to have a very sudden finish.

"So," said O, "The wine that you are now drinking is different from the wine at... that other place?"

"Dramatically so. Night and day. Suppose that you had been in a cave, with only torchlight, and you emerged into the late evening sun, with a bit of cloudiness: That time of beautiful light that artists call 'the golden hour.' That would be this wine.

"And by comparison with this, suppose that you were in a dark and air-conditioned hotel room, wearing a blindfold, and you stepped out into the noonday sun of the Algerian desert, with not so much as a cloud in the sky. As you ripped the blindfold from your eyes, that is how Xino Chymo would be compared to this that we now sip with our meal."

"That seems a bit over-dramatic," said Millie. "I mean, this tastes better than that did, but, really, it's just wine."

Johns resisted the urge to tell her that she had the palate of a goat. He instead smiled and politely said, "Yes, well, there you are."

Millie grimaced and glanced at him from the corners of her eye. She had the impression that he was making fun of her.

They ate in relative silence. Johns could not speak to them about the matter at hand, for fear of being overheard, and he had no rapport with Millie, to allow them to converse casually. From time to time, Johns would point out a person passing by – the café seemed to be a main traffic route from the organs of the hotel to the backstage areas.

"Jackson," said a large stocky man, whose thin black hair had been carefully combed over the bald crown of his head. "I don't believe that I know your guests." He gave them a smile that was clearly not the normal expression of his rounded face. It was the smile of a man whose teeth hurt, or who was about to politely apply his professional power to repel an interloper. "Oleg Rustoff," he said, offering a hand across the table to O.

"O Johnson," said O. shaking the offered hand. It was a businessman's handshake: firm enough, but without pressure; soft enough, and yet not relaxed. O noted the man's suit: medium gray chalk stripe, neither brand new nor visibly worn, carefully and precisely fitted. No vest.

Medium gray made this man a director or senior manager. It was not so dark as to command attention. Top executives and the most junior salesmen wear black, all others wear gray. It was also not so light as to blend into the fog, a common color for middle managers who did not wish to draw attention to themselves as individuals.

A muted blue tie in a regimental stripe pattern. Again, subtle. Junior managers might have a humorous twist to their pattern, or wear a yellow foulard in hopes of being noticed by the brass, but this man clearly had no concerns. He was who he needed to be, and those who needed to know him already knew him.

Of course, in the UK, he might be challenged for the right to wear a regimental stripe. Here, it was merely a design; there it indicated actual membership in a certain regiment. There, he would do better with paisley.

The man and his painful smile turned to Millie.

"Millicent Millford," she said with a haughty tone, giving him the look of a woman asked to hold a rotten codfish. O noted that the suit repulsed her. Clearly, Millie had no patience for corporate America and its conventions.

"My cousins from California," explained Johns. "I'm just showing them around."

"Very good," said Rustoff, the smile slipping from his face. "We'll need to review the inventory later. Come see me in your office when your guests leave." O wondered if reviewing the inventory was a code to tell Jackson that the wine currently on the table would come out of Jackson's commissions.

Rustoff turned the painful smile back on and waved his hand over the table. "Nice to meet you," he said, turning his back and strolling down the corridor.

"Meet it is I set it down," said Johns under his breath.

Millie glared at him. Obviously, he was showing up her ignorance by saying something so obscure. What a mean little man. Pretentious about his thousand dollar wines, and snippy with his private-school one-liners.

O merely nodded and cut into his lemon chicken. "A man may smile and smile," he replied.

"What do you think?" asked O, as they cruised over the narrow bridge that connected Hotel Island and the Inn at River Columbia to Cape Disappointment. The sun dipped low, far to their left, making long shadows of the trees and the old Cape Disappointment lighthouse. The mists that had dampened their southward run were returning, and offered to call down the rain.

"Pretentious drunken snob," blurted Millie. "Nearly passed out over the crème bruleé."

"About the wine," clarified O.

"Oh. Well, the second stuff was much better," declared Millie.

"I mean the replacements. The theft," exclaimed O.

"Oh. Yeah, there's probably something going on."

It's like pulling teeth, thought O. "So how would someone systematically get wine from the cellar, open it, replace it, recork it, and put it back into the cellar?"

"Easier from that fridge in the restaurant," said Millie. "The one with the glass front."

"Those are the more common wines," said O. "The expensive ones don't come out of the cellar until they're being sold."

"I think that salmon he gave me was bad."

"Are you feeling sick?"

"No, but my stomach hurts."

"Need me to stop somewhere?"

"No, but drive faster."

They drove in silence for a while. She put one hand on her stomach, and then after a while added the second one. The look on her face transitioned through mild annoyance, a distinct grimace, and was progressing towards outright misery when O spoke again.

"I'm stopping at Nemah," he said. "They've got to have some kind of medical facility."

"They don't," she said, through clenched teeth. "It's on to South Bend or back down and over to Astoria. Keep going."

"Nothing in Ilwaco?"

"One place, but my step-sister worked there. And I wouldn't give her the satisfaction. So no, there's nothing. Just go faster."

O had to admit that the blend of marshes and forests, flying past in an endless procession, did not bode well for finding aid. He kept an eye for a glimmer of light through the drizzle, to indicate some sort of business, but he saw only trees. He pressed down harder on the accelerator.

"You'll tell me if you're going to be sick," said O, but it was a question disguised as a statement. She waved a dismissive hand at him and went back to cradling her stomach with her arms.

O started looking for a gas station. Or maybe a fire house. Or anywhere he could stop and call for an ambulance. He did not want responsibility for a sick person. Especially if, as it looked to his untrained eye, she was in some desperate sort of distress.

Roads darted off to the left and to the right, but none of them looked promising. Without a better knowledge of the area, he could wind up at a deserted farmhouse or a dead end. Or he might get lost on side roads while his ephemeral companion went into deadly convulsive spasms.

He racked his brain, trying to remember the trip south. Was there any place at all where there might be help? He couldn't remember any; just an endless parade of trees and sloughs and backwaters. A house here or there, a barn, a metal warehouse. No place that guaranteed help.

His foot pressed harder on the accelerator. The only safe thing to do was to get her to South Bend, and the faster the better. The pavement was damp, but the tire paths were dry from other cars, and there was no danger of hydroplaning.

Millie rocked in her seat as he went around a curve.

"Hey," she said. "Slow down, you'll make me sick!"

"I think that's inevitable," he said, but he eased off, from flagrant abuse of the speed limit to mere reckless disregard. The two-lane highway poured by under his wheels, and the road began to hiss as his tires spun up moisture off the road.

It crossed his mind to wonder if the glovebox maybe had some kind of plastic bag, or something she could use as a sickness bag if the need arose suddenly. Probably not, he decided, so he instead kept watch for wide shoulders he could use for an emergency stop.

It was about twenty more minutes into South Bend, but it seemed like hours. O brought the old Coronet to a stop right behind Langer's patrol car, and jumped out of the driver's seat to open Millie's door. Millie was leaning back, groaning, breathing in through the corners of her mouth and pushing her breath out through pursed lips.

Langer stuck his head out the door of the sheriff's office.

"You can't park there!" he shouted.

"Millie's sick," yelled O. "We need an ambulance!"

Langer started to yell back, then thought better of it and stepped back inside. Moments later he returned with a red nylon case and trotted carefully to the car with one hand on his left shirt pocket, in the cautious way that middle-aged men run.

"What's wrong with her?" said Langer.

"Stomach," said O. "She was complaining of an upset stomach, then muscle pain, and now she's not even speaking."

"Where does it hurt?" asked Langer, and Millie replied by staring at him with a look of raw hatred. Clearly, that was the wrong question.

Millie, for her part, was trying to imagine how a man might be elected Sheriff when he couldn't immediately understand that she had clearly been poisoned. She was dying, and he was asking inane questions. Where did it hurt? Honestly?

"I should call down to that hotel in Ilwaco," said O. "We had lunch with a man down there. He might be feeling the same way."

A deputy, whom O hadn't yet met, stuck his head out the door of the office, watching in abject horror. Sheriff Langer pawed through the first aid bag, looking for something he could safely give Millie. But without knowing what was bothering her…

Well, thought Langer, *At least it's not Cyanide. She'd be dead already, like that woman from the hotel.* He immediately regretted thinking that. It really hadn't been a laughing matter, and when it was all over he had been relieved to think that his one-murder-every-two-years was paid up until 2023. But if Millie had been poisoned also, that would ruin his stats completely. And he regretted thinking that, also.

He found a packet of activated charcoal in the bag, and he vaguely remembered that it could be used to absorb poison. He ripped open the packet – about an ounce, he supposed – and flicked it with his index finger to break it up. A tiny cloud of fine powder wafted from the top of the packet. He pressed the edge to open it wide.

"Here, Millie," he said, holding out the charcoal. "Swallow this. It'll make you feel better."

Millie paused in her huffing and puffing to tilt her head slightly and open her mouth. He had poured perhaps half an ounce when she closed her lips and sputtered. She raised her head as he took away the pouch. There was soot all over her chin.

Her eyes would have reproved him for this horrible trick — pouring that dry stuff into her mouth — but she had to swallow to get the charcoal down so she could yell at him. And she couldn't swallow because the charcoal made her mouth dry.

For about three or four minutes, she worked her lips and licked at the roof of her mouth like a dog eating peanut butter. She swallowed at last, and Langer offered her a small bottle of water. She used it to wash down the charcoal.

Then suddenly her eyes swelled, and she leaned towards Langer. He read her motion accurately and jumped backwards just in time. The effluent was black with charcoal, giving the whole thing a ghastly and surreal feel.

O came back out of the office and saw her leaning out of the car, retching into the puddle of black bile. He suddenly felt very light-headed. A distant siren heralded the imminent ambulance. He sat down quickly, squatting on the ground. He didn't expect it to help, but it would make his fall less harmful when he passed out.

Sitting down did make him feel better, so he rested his hands on his knees and braced his forehead between his thumbs.

"You too?" asked Langer. "You guys eat poison sumac salad or something, down there?"

"Not poisoned," said O. "It's… nerves. Just nerves." He opened his eyes and raised his head to look up at the Sheriff. "I'm fine. Nerves is all."

Langer glanced over at Millie, who was using one hand to keep herself from falling out of the car. He supposed that it made sense for O to worry about her. But why the hell hadn't he pulled over and phoned it in?

Oleg Rustoff drummed his fingers on his desk. Who would have known that a professional drunk like Jackson Johns had relatives? They looked nothing like him, but cousins might not. He debated how much to make Johns pay over the wine. On the one hand, a trip to the cellar and a meal on the house – those were perquisites that came with the territory. As a senior manager, Johns had it coming. He needed to be familiar with the products, and familiarity came through frequent sampling. It would be written off as professional training and quality control, of course. And compared to other things…

Well. Best not to think about what it might be compared to.

The real problem was that Johns seemed different lately. Inquisitive. Troubled. A bit too concerned about the paperwork, a little too interested in the invoices and receipts for the wines. With only six months until the change of management, this was no time for Johns to be counting corks.

The upcoming change of management would be a good excuse for a complete inventory of the cellar. It would have to be done after the restaurant closed, to keep from accidentally counting the same bottle twice, or missing a bottle in transit. Johns would be down there all night long. Plenty of time for Oleg and Kurt to sort things out.

"So apparently it works like this: The hotel buys cheap wine, and sells expensive wine. There's a bit of rebottling and re-labeling that takes place in between." O looked around the waiting room, with too-bright lights reflecting from too-white walls.

"So the hotel makes money. Which means that the whole management crew is in on it." Langer spoke on whispers, carefully looking around to make sure they were not overheard.

"Not necessarily. Only a handful of the managers ever get to see the raw financial data. And even fewer could ever compare it against invoices. Usually one person handles AP, and another does AR, and the controller is the only one who sees the trial ledgers."

"AP? AR? What's that?"

"Accounts payable – that's the money that's going out of the hotel – and accounts receivable – that's the money coming in."

"Oh, right. But that kind of a scam, like you were talking about – selling bad wine as good – that doesn't directly benefit anyone on the staff. Just the hotel's bottom line."

"Well, it's entirely possible that there's some laundry involved. The money from the sales goes in as F&B revenue, but then…"

"F and B?"

"Food and beverage. Any restaurant or room service sales. So it's mingled into the general revenue stream, and then later it gets paid out as an unexpected and unpredictable expense. Like broken crockery, that was one he mentioned. Johns, I mean."

"So they cheat customers in order to buy extra plates."

"Except that the plates never arrive. There are two invoices for each order. One invoice has a real price that corresponds to real merchandise – that's the one that the vendor keeps."

"The other gets turned in to the hotel's accountants."

"Right, and it's way too high, and lists way too much stuff. But it lets the hotel managers prove that the money went to crockery. We broke a lot of dishes that month; a steward tripped going down some stairs. We couldn't match the pattern of the old plates. So we replaced it all, and look, here's the invoice."

"Okay, but that still doesn't benefit the managers."

"It does when the vendor sends that manager a consulting fee. Personally, to his home address. Or a finder's fee, or maybe a sales commission. Or possibly just hands him an envelope full of cash."

"Ah. A nice little side income, neatly laundered."

"Of course the vendor keeps a cut, but that's a small price for clean money, neatly pressed with extra starch."

Langer smoothed his mustache with a thumb and forefinger, from the center outward. He wasn't sure that he completely got it, but he would spend some time thinking about it.

A doctor came through the double doors, and both men stood to meet him. The doctor made a beeline for the Sheriff.

"We ran a tox scan on the sputum, and also on the effluent from the gastric lavage," he said.

Langer raised an eyebrow and looked at O.

"They pumped her stomach and tested what came out," said O, with a shrug.

"Right. We didn't find any common toxins or any indications of food poisoning." The doctor frowned. "But we did find quite a bit of acetylsalicylic acid."

"Aspirin," said O.

"Yes. Is she on an aspirin regimen?"

Langer and O shrugged at each other.

"We really have no way of knowing," said Langer.

"Low pH?" asked O.

"Low end of normal," said the doctor. "Apparently she had eaten a meal a couple hours earlier?"

"We had lunch in Ilwaco," said O. "So, maybe four hours ago? You're thinking a peptic ulcer?"

A cloud passed across the doctor's face. "We'll do some more tests. I really shouldn't be talking about it with you."

"But there's no reason to worry?" asked Langer.

"She's stable," said the doctor. "We'll keep her overnight and discharge her in the morning. Oh, and who gave her the charcoal?"

"I did," said Langer.

"Next time call us first. It didn't hurt her, but it made a real mess out of the gastric lavage." He turned and walked away.

"Made a mess out of a gastric lavage." snorted Langer, under his breath. "Bet it made a hole in the ground out of a copper mine."

For the first time in maybe six months, O had the dream.

It started in the men's room, washing his hands. He was watching himself, as if the memory were a movie, and at the same time he was the man standing, washing his hands in cold water. The distant part of his mind thought it was odd; his hands didn't even have blood on them yet.

He dried them with a paper towel and reached for the door handle. As an observer, he begged himself not to open the door. He told himself to hide. But the memory didn't hear him. He eased the door open and stepped into the bank lobby.

Behind the bank robbers.

In his countless retellings to the police and to a therapist, he had named them One, Two, and Three. Killer One had positioned himself near the ATM, across the lobby from the other two. His AK-47 was still partially hidden by the heavy hunting jacket. Killer Two was directly in front of O, already holding the shotgun in plain view, at a relaxed port arms position. Killer Three was to the left of Two. O couldn't tell where he held his AK, and in the end, it didn't matter at all.

O's rational mind struggled to take it in, but his limbic mind acted on its own. He tugged the pistol from Two's waist and drew on One, dropping him with a single shot. The AK-47 fell from under his jacket, clattering on the ground.

The shot startled Two, and he jerked the shotgun trigger, putting a load of double-ought buckshot through the ear of Three. Three crumpled into a heap on the white tile floor.

O stumbled back as Two pivoted, already racking the slide of the shotgun. O shot him three times at point blank range, each shot deadly on its own. Two, after a millisecond that seemed like eternity, fell facedown at O's feet.

For a moment they all stared at him: all of the bank employees and all of the customers. They were half-hunched over, covering their ears, and staring in open-mouthed shock and horror at the man holding a gun, who had just killed three people. Staring at him.

He knew that his own eyes mirrored theirs: Wide and terrified. He dropped the gun, letting it fall onto the tile floor. He held out his hands to show that he wasn't armed. He was no danger to anyone. He was safe as kittens.

Sirens outside were growing louder. People were staring at him in horror. He needed to explain, but there were no words.

And then he snapped awake in a cold sweat.

While the coffee perked, he thought about the dream. He didn't want to, but he really had no choice. What frightened him most was that he had acted without thinking. What if they had been security guards, or undercover policemen, or hunters with a poor understanding of when to use open carry? What if he had killed three innocent men for no good reason? Why couldn't he have taken half a second to understand before he acted?

He knew why not. Had he hesitated for even a millisecond, the shotgun would have taken down the security guard, and the AKs would have flooded the room with a deadly cross-fire. Then they would have seen him, and shot him. And even if he had cowered in the men's room, they would have found him and shot him. Any other action, anything at all, would have been suicide. And a dozen other innocent people, or even more, would have died as well.

He made the right choice; that was undeniable. Everyone called him a hero. But he had used the wrong process. He reacted instead of thinking. And now his brain kept making him think about it, like a punishment for the earlier omission. Sometimes he would go weeks between dreams; other times he'd see it several times in one night.

Strong coffee and crossword puzzles kept him awake until dawn, when the sunrise brought the relative safety of day.

The dream was worse the second night. The bank robbers weren't robbers at all. They were security guards, policemen, hunters with carry permits. And each time he cut them down without thinking, without pausing to assess.

The last time, they weren't armed at all. In place of One stood Millie Millie the Misanthrope, red wine pouring from the holes he shot into her. Her face registered contempt, that he could do such a thing. And to her, of all people.

Two and Three merged into Triple-A, and she looked at him with surprise and betrayal. The look she gave him told of deep pain beyond the physical injury itself: She had thought they were friends. She had expected better from him.

Stronger coffee kept him awake for the rest of that night and into the day. On the third night, he took sleeping pills and dreamed no dreams, or none that he remembered.

O walked into the Sheriff's office unshaven and looking slightly hung over. The look had nothing to do with alcohol, and everything to do with several nights of deep, drug-induced sleep.

"Millie's going to be okay," said triple-A, in way of a greeting, when she saw him in the hallway. "But she's supposed to take it easy for a few weeks."

O nodded to her and made his way to the break room.

There was a stranger at the break-room table, where Millie had been at the last meeting. She peered through bifocals at knitting that rose from her lap. She nodded at him, but her eyes didn't leave the needlework.

"Shelley Colfax," she said, without dropping a stitch. "You must be the new fellow on the team."

"Call me O," he said, expecting the usual dialog about it. To his surprise, she merely nodded.

"Heard Millie keeled over on you," she said. Her tone was slightly jovial, and didn't match the solemn face.

"Stomach thing," said O, pouring himself a cup of coffee in a tiny paper cup. The coffee was too hot, so he added a second cup as an insulator.

"Where you from, Joe?"

"Dunsmuir," he said. "Though I was born in Idaho and raised in Santa Barbara."

"Santa Barbara." she nodded. "Grandaughter went to college there." With that, Shelley was talking about colleges, and someone her granddaughter knew, and a situation involving an apartment and a landlord who was very strict. Not at all 420-friendly, you understand, which was fine, but he was quite adamant, you see… O was able to disengage his mind and allow the words to flow past him as she told the tale.

He did note, almost without realizing it, that she was running on about a topic while complaining about a man running on about a topic. It was oddly recursive.

The string of chatter, with an occasional grunt from O, went on for almost twenty minutes before Millie walked in.

"We have a new case," she said, putting the folder on the table between the three of them.

"I thought you were in the hospital," said Shelley. "Are you up to being out and about?" She stopped knitting, and gave the Millie her full attention.

"I'm fine," she said. "Bit of an upset stomach. Bad fish."

Langer chose that moment to walk in. "O, I need to see you when you're done here. Millie, good to see you up and around."

"No thanks to you," she snapped. "Nearly poisoned me with that charcoal powder."

"Sorry," said Langer, raising his hands and backing out of the room. Millie stared at his retreat for a moment before sliding photocopied sheets of paper to the other two.

O glanced down at it. Last June – and it was currently October? – Mrs. Diane Fletcher had seen two men smoking cigarettes by the Circle-K and talking to her teen-aged daughter Arinae. That night, Arinae disappeared without a trace.

"This happened here in South Bend?" asked O.

Shelley nodded and lowered her knitting. "For teenager, read nineteen-going-on-thirty."

O skimmed the rest of the document. The clerk in the Circle-K described the men as being in their late teens, and one of them had tried to buy beer with a fake ID. The clerk was very clear – two entire paragraphs, as summarized in the reports – that he had not sold them any liquor, would not sell them any liquor, never ever sold liquor to under-aged customers, and had no idea where they had gotten the cigarettes.

"This clerk, how well does his story hold up?" asked O.

"He didn't contradict himself, and the security tapes at the store only show the three standing by the payphone outside for a while. The two males have their back to the camera," stated Millie.

"The Circle-K has a pay-phone?"

"Well, the stand where it used to be."

"Height, weight estimates?"

"Not from those cameras," said Shelley. "They barely even focus. They only keep them there as a bluff. Useless for law enforcement."

O looked at the blown-up still from the cameras, and saw her point. The black and white photos were grainy and out of focus, with a stripe of static across the legs of the three youths. The interior photo was slightly better, but the camera only showed the top of the youth's head. It had been pointed virtually straight down, at the register, as if the point were to keep the clerk honest.

"So we know that she met with two young men outside the store. Was she seen later?"

"Her mother said she came home and apparently went to bed. But her bed hadn't been slept in, and some of her clothes were gone. Also, several personal possessions were missing. No sign of forced entry or any struggle at the house."

"Runaway," said O. "Well, no, she's legally an adult and she can go where she wants. Missing clothes, no struggle – wherever she went, it sounds like she went willingly. She's probably working at a food cart over in Portland."

"Her mother disagrees, and she hasn't stopped complaining. She's demanding that we take some kind of action," said Shelley. "The sheriff probably gave us the case just so he could say he's doing something."

"We should probably interview this Diane – "

"Dee-Ahn-Eh," said Shelley. "She pronounces it DNA."

"Ah," said O.

"And the daughter is RNA. Ar, In, Eh." There was a twinkle in Shelley's eye, and O wasn't sure if it was an expression of small-town contempt for the mis-named mother and daughter, or if it was amusement at the genetic joke. He decided to ignore it.

"So, ah, we should speak with the, ah, with Di-an-e… ah, just to let her know we're on the case…"

"I'll do that," said Millie. "It'll let me explain why I missed bridge last week." Millie glared towards Langer's office, as if the missed bridge game were his fault.

"Silly question: Did anyone try to contact these two young men?" asked O.

Millie narrowed her eyes at him, but Shelley answered first. "They were never positively identified, and all the young men who look like that have claimed not to have seen her."

"Strangers, then? Might be a good lead if we can identify them." O shrugged. "Just a thought. I mean, she might have left town with them. It's about the only lead we have."

The meeting ended abruptly, as Millie picked up her manila folder, and Shelley gathered her knitting. O slipped out of the break room and headed for Langer's office.

The sheriff looked up from his paperwork and nodded to a chair by his desk.

"This wine thing has me stumped," he said, without preamble. "I don't know a thing about wine, and I don't understand those people down at that hotel. It's like they're from a different planet."

"I see," said O, though he really didn't.

"Two years ago we had a couple of murders down there, and I used some detectives from California to get it resolved. I didn't care much for the way they worked, but they got the job done. Any chance you'd reach out to them?"

"Um, just to be clear: Millie said that we weren't supposed to work open cases."

"You're not, not as the civilian review board. But this is out of my wheelhouse. I need someone who sees things differently. That's what I've always respected about you, O. You cut through the muck and address the problem straight on."

"Okay…"

"So I'm going to ask for you to do me a one-time favor. I'm invoking *Posse Comitatus*."

"You're deputizing a posse to defend the county? Over a few bottles of wine?"

"I'm deputizing you, as a posse of one. I'm asking you to face one specific emergency, namely, whatever the hell is going on down at that hotel."

"I can't carry a gun. I mean, I won't." O shook his head. "I'm not even sure that this is legal."

"It's within existing precedent. The law says that a sheriff, or even a magistrate, can call out local citizens to defend the county. It doesn't say how many or how few. If this went before a court, I might get challenged on the public outcry clause, but I think I can swing it, if it comes to that. And it won't."

"What do I tell..."

"Millie and Shelley? Not a thing. This is on the QT. As for a gun, if you want to, buy one. *Posse Comitatus* can, by definition, carry open or concealed. But you don't have to."

"What am I supposed to do?"

"Something stinks on that little island. I want you to tell me what it is, and then I'll root it out. That's all."

Chapter Four

"KURT, WE HAVE AN issue."

Kurt Foulard looked up from the papers on his desk, into the face of Oleg Rustoff. Rustoff had closed the door of Foulard's office. Clearly, it was not for the ears of the secretaries in the outer offices. He leaned back and crossed his legs.

Rustoff, without invitation, drew up a chair and sat near the desk, across from Foulard.

"It's Johns. I think he's onto us."

"Onto us. You think he knows…"

"About the wine, at the very least."

Foulard relaxed. "He's a drunk. We'll write him up for being drunk on duty, give him a suspension, and then claim that he's trying to get even with us."

"It's not that simple. He was talking to some people. He said they were his cousins. He gave them lunch in the café."

"Wine?"

"He and the woman shared a Castel Não Beber. It's not that expensive. I won't charge it to him."

"Big deal. They're relatives. They don't know anything."

"If he told them about the wine, it might look bad later."

"They can't prove when he told them what. We can still claim it's just Johns getting back at us for firing him for being a drunk. And when we fire him…"

"Right, we set him up as the patsy for everything else. Of course. I'm with you, but I wanted you to know."

"We'll call him in tonight and give him a formal warning, just to get the paperwork started. I'm thinking we should walk in, maybe surprise him in that little nest he keeps up at the top of the stairs. The old HVAC storage room."

Oleg grinned. "I couldn't think of a better setting for it."

O felt very out of place. The haircut left his ears feeling cold, and shaving off his mustache made his upper lip feel prickly. He kept resisting the urge to touch his philtrum, to feel where the mustache had been.

"Mister… Johnson?" asked the lady behind the desk.

"Yes," he said. "My name is Vowel, but I prefer to be called Al. It leads to fewer questions about my first name."

"Al Johnson. That will be fine. I see that you worked in a bank before this."

"Yes," he replied. "I had some issues, a bit of a breakdown. I had to leave."

"You're not currently under a doctor's care?"

"No, no, not at all. I'm fit as a fiddle. I just, well, there were some stressful things. In my personal life. That's why I moved up here, to get away from all that."

"And you checked that we should not contact them for a reference."

"No, um… Well, when I had my breakdown … It wasn't a good thing. I said some things, did some things – it was the stress, you understand."

"But you have local references?"

"Yes. Shelley Colfax, up in South Bend, she's an old friend." O assuaged his conscience by noting that Shelley was both a friend and also old. So it wasn't a lie. Not really. "And Jackson Johns, he's a distant cousin."

Preferring to be called Al, as opposed to Vowel, well, that also wasn't a lie – anything was preferable to his given name. He had never called himself Al before, but it seemed like a plausible substitute, and it was unremarkable.

Unremarkable was good.

The woman looked him over, gazing at him with a judicious eye. On the one hand, his resumé was a little thin, and the story of a breakdown at a bank... it was a bit sketchy. Her first instinct was to decline and move on.

But he knew Jackson, and Jackson was a solid, long term employee. Also, she desperately needed stewards. It wasn't easy to find people who wanted to work all night long pushing plastic trays of cups and plates through a hot steamy dishwasher in a hot steamy kitchen. And the pay left a lot to be desired, as well.

Furthermore, it was mindless work; no stress that was likely to invoke further breakdowns. Besides, if he tried to claim workman's comp later on, she could point to the pre-existing condition. So it was a fairly small risk.

"Alright," she conceded. "Can you start tonight?"

For his part, O had assessed the human resources woman as well. Not physically, but he did note her dark brown eyes, her long, curly brown hair, and her gentle, subtle features. When she smiled – a purely professional smile, he was certain – her eyes turned into inverted smiles. When she didn't, they looked like dots.

She was pretty – he noted it academically – but not his type. And it was never a good idea to ask out the HR analyst.

Becka Corwallis stood at the front desk, idly staring out the window while she waited for someone, anyone, to wander up and try to check in. She couldn't believe that she was back here, but where else would she go? This was the place she knew; the place where she had friends. And for a woman with a small daughter, that was an important qualifier.

She had met Ben here. So there was that. She couldn't hold it against the hotel that she and Ben didn't work out. Whatever his faults, the man could cook, at least, so it made sense that he had been well liked here. But the sous-chefs who loved him here ... they hadn't had to live with him. Or try to raise children with him.

Steve Sauer was still here. She liked working with Steve. If he wasn't married, she might have liked getting to know him a little better. But all the good ones were taken. It always worked that way.

38

At least Leon was gone. Leon Rothenberg, the former Rooms Division Manager, had left not long after the two murders. About the time she had run off to Dallas with Ben. There was something about Leon – He hadn't been creepy, or anything like that, but there was something about him that told her not to trust him.

Kurt Foulard was still the General Manager, and that man did give her the creeps. He seemed to think that the hotel was his personal kingdom. She had always half-expected him to hit on her at any given time. Fortunately, he never had.

And his wife Vanity – she was a real piece of work, wasn't she? Becka hadn't run into her since returning from Dallas, but it was inevitable. Becka wasn't looking forward to it.

Well, life at the Inn on River Columbia was no bed of roses, but at least it was better than being married to Ben. And in time life would go back to normal. It just had to.

Steve Sauer was on time, as usual. He needed the job, so he showed up on time, did what needed to be done, and went home. It was a compromise job: He was capable of working in better positions for better pay, but he needed a job that meshed with his wife's schedule. One of them needed to see their son off to school, and one of them needed to be there when he came home.

So Steve took the evening shift.

He waved to Becka as he went past the front desk and into the back office. She smiled. He was glad to see her back, though he was a bit surprised. She and Ben had seemed so right for each other.

He reported in at Oleg Rustoff's office. Since Leon's abrupt departure, Oleg had taken over his office, in every sense of the phrase. It wasn't uncommon to see him shuttling between the Room Division Manager's office and the Food and Beverage Office. Steve wasn't sure if they were planning to hire a new Rooms Manager, or if Rustoff would simply do both jobs indefinitely.

He hoped that they were hiring. The change in the work environment alone – a real professional for a manager, instead of the inter-connected schemers who normally got promoted around the hotel – would be worth the process of proving himself to a new manager. And there was even the possibility that he might be able to claim the job for himself. He'd get a decent salary for a change, his wife wouldn't have to work, and he could be home nearly every evening. Well, once he found someone to be the night manager.

That thought; the idea of escaping this job by taking a promotion – it brought a bit of light to an otherwise hopeless shift on a job that was going absolutely nowhere.

Millie Millie was fuming. O seemed to be taking over the Volunteer Civilian Review Board. He had practically run the last meeting, and then he simply announced that the girl had run off with her friends. He totally dismissed her thoughts on it. Honestly? No investigation? None at all?

What was Millie going to tell Diane?

Millie and Diane went way back, to before even high school. They had cut classes together, shared cigarettes, and gone through the entire juvenile rebellion stage as comrades in arms. Sure, Diane could be a little bit dramatic about things. Deep down, Millie had to admit that Arinae was probably fine, and was likely shacked up with one of the guys from the convenience store pictures.

But they could at least go through the motions, and pretend to look for her. Shelley was probably already telling everyone how O had simply dismissed the disappearance, just like that. And how silly and stupid Diane and her mother were.

She hadn't missed the winks between O and Shelley, over the way the mother and daughter pronounced their names. O was probably doubled over in laughter, right this minute, making fun of Millie's old friend.

Jackson Johns was filled with a sense of foreboding. That wasn't uncommon these days. He often felt a vague dread about going in to work, but he usually assuaged it with a glass of wine, put on his best smile, and dove in head-first.

Tonight was different. Tonight, he felt like he was actually in danger. Real, palpable, present, tangible danger. It was lurking up in the restaurant; it was hiding down in the wine cellar. He hadn't been this frightened since the time he had kicked open the wine cellar and discovered Kurt lurking down there, locked in through his own ignorance. And even that was over in a flash, as soon as he realized that the interloper was merely the General Manager.

It was a matter of time, he knew it. He had to leave the hotel. He couldn't keep doing this. He had nowhere else to go, and he had carved out a comfortable spot for himself here. Or it had been, until the current administration. He would have to quit very soon, whether he found another job or not. It was inevitable.

But for tonight, for now, he had to keep going. He felt compelled, predestined, fated to go to work. Fated to face the dragons that awaited him.

He quaffed the dregs of the wine, and sent himself to work.

Chapter Five

O WAITED FOR THE green plastic rack of glassware to
come out of the dragon. It slid through the strips of black rubber
that formed the final curtain, allowing wisps of steam to escape as it
did. O grabbed the rack and swung it into place atop a stack of
similar green racks, behind him.

The stack of green racks rose shoulder high, and behind it
were several more. Each stack, once it had cooled and the last
droplets of water had dripped from it, would be systematically
stripped of its cargo. The glassware and flatware would be stacked
in the cages behind the cold line and salad prep areas.

O had no idea how many plates, bowls, and glasses of various
sizes and shapes were stacked there, but it had to number in the
hundreds, if not thousands. A part of his mind dared him to count
them; another part declared the exercise silly and pointless.

He stepped back, his green plasticized apron slapping against
his legs. Three good steps took him up to the front of the dragon,
where another three trays sat at the pre-rinse station. He seized the
stainless steel hose that hung over the sink, squeezed the lever to
spray each individual glass, turned them all face down, and fed the
first tray into the dragon's front end.

Lather, Rinse, Repeat, he thought, as the next two trays vanished into the dishwasher. The first one was already triggering the final rinse arm. He could hear the hiss of the almost-boiling water.

That was the last tray, and he looked around the kitchen for anything else that needed to be cleaned. The pots and pans were gone from the cooking line; the hotel trays had been cleared out of the steam tables, and all of the counter tops had been wiped down. As soon as the last three trays of glassware were stacked up and left to dry, his work would be done.

Last of all, he shut down the dragon, stepping on the foot-levers to drain its tanks, flipping the switches to kill its water heaters, and turning off the soap dispensers. The kitchen became eerily silent.

Night cleaners would come in later, so he left all the lights on. They would scrub the floors, clean the rubber fatigue mats at the cooking lines, and steam the grease catchers on the massive exhaust hoods that overshadowed the cooktops.

In the morning, the early stewards would put away the dishes that O had just cleaned, and lay out the items needed for breakfast. O stood for a moment, mesmerized by the stillness and silence.

A swinging door opened, and a server walked through. She was a slender young woman in black slacks and a white long-sleeved shirt. O knew her. From where?

He had to blink a couple of times to place her, but he knew her. The photo. The mole beneath one ear, the smallish nose, the dimples. It was Arinae Fletcher.

His first thought was that he couldn't tell Millie. She'd hate him if he found Arinae so easily. He liked solving puzzles, but it really was not his goal to make everyone else look stupid. He'd have to ignore her for a couple of days, while he confirmed her identity. But it was her.

"Hey," she said. "Are you new?"

"Yeah. Call me Al." He started to offer a hand, but the big rubber gloves made that impossible.

She laughed. "Good to meet you, Al. I'm Rina."

O smiled. She had dropped the first syllable and shortened the last, giving herself a less distinctive name. And by that simple trick, she had fallen completely off the map.

O made a deduction about her mother's assumptions, but didn't say it out loud. It was a pointless observation, like many of the facts that lodged within his mind. "That's an unusual name," he said, instead. He didn't intend to start a conversation, but he knew very well that unusual names warranted a remark. To omit such a remark would almost be rude.

"Yes," she said, with a private laugh, nearly silent. "Yes, it is."

"What keeps you so late?"

"Folding napkins. Side work. You know."

"Ah," said O. She might have replied as she walked past, and if so, it was something glib and whimsical that didn't require an answer. As quickly as that, she was out the back door and gone.

O hung up his apron and shook his hands out of the huge gloves. He felt damp. Earlier, the steam from the dragon had made him feel hot and muggy; now the condensation on his clothing was giving him a chill.

He clocked out, and then remembered one last errand. He didn't bother to clock back in.

The swinging doors from the kitchen put him into a large coffee-service area, generally known as the bus station. One end of it was dominated by glass-front refrigerators, filled with wine bottles. The opposite end was a complete coffee bar, from espresso machine to sugar-packets. In between were shelves with every condiment known to mankind.

The second set of swinging doors put him into the tasting room. It was a large, square room, with glass wine racks serving as two of its sides. Beyond the glass racks, across the dining room proper, huge windows showed the blackness of night. In the daytime, one would see the mouth of the Columbia River, as it opened into the Pacific Ocean. At night, as now, the blackness was broken only by the rocks below, lit by powerful lights on the rooftop above the restaurant.

The two walls opposite the ocean were also covered in wine racks, but these were wooden and gave no hint of the wonders beyond. A narrow doorway opened into a short, dark passage, presenting the offices of the Executive Chef and of the Food and Beverage Manager. At the end of the passage was a solid wooden door with a panic bar.

O pushed the panic bar, and the door opened into the well-lit lobby, near the front doors. He let it close behind him, noting, not for the first time, how completely the door disappeared into the wooden paneling when closed.

The clerk looked up as he walked to the front desk. Her eyes asked how she might help him.

"Al," he said, by way of introduction. "I'm the new steward. Apparently I'm supposed to check for dishes up here before I leave for the night?"

Becka smiled at him. "Nothing to declare, Al," she said. "I had a valet take them through a couple hours ago."

"Great," he said. He let himself out the front doors and disappeared into the dark.

The dream, this time, was different. The dragon, partly a steaming dishwasher and partly a Chinese festival costume, was rampaging through the bank lobby, knocking over customers and upsetting the marble tables for filling out deposit slips. Millie Millie was trying to get it under control, spraying the room with bullets. But the wily dragon dodged, steaming and hissing, while Millie Millie turned her AK-47 from side to side, shots snapping like firecrackers in a New Year's parade.

At last, the dragon fell down, but it was too late. All the bank customers and the tellers were dead, riddled with bullets. Millie turned to him, eyes blazing.

"This is all your fault," she said, pointing to his chest. He looked down, and he was bleeding from dozens of small holes.

He snapped awake.

He was in a tiny loft in Ilwaco. It was a cheap rental; something to give him a local address. Langer had wanted him to commute, but felt that he needed to be in the community to understand the community. Not that there was much of a community, and the hotel people tended to commute in from Astoria, anyway..

It was an A-frame garage, and his landlords' cars were visible below him. The loft covered the back half of the garage, giving him just enough room for a small bed, a chair, and a table with a microwave oven. It wasn't much, but it came cheaply.

He stood up and walked to the railing, gazing idly down on the cars below. It wasn't much of a life, washing dishes and sleeping in a garage. And his real life up in South Bend wasn't much better. But at least he was finally doing something constructive.

He put a cup of water into the microwave, along with a teabag-style coffee filter. Two minutes on high. He spent the rest of the night drinking mediocre coffee and working crossword puzzles.

Seven across: the debt all men must pay. That was an easy clue. It came from Euripides, and the answer was death. He took a moment to think, not for the first time, about the deaths in the bank. Why did they still give him bad dreams, after all this time? They were bad men. They deserved... well, that is, if there was ever anyone who deserved to die, it was killers like those.

So what kept him from just getting over it? Was it fear that he had misjudged them? That they were really nice guys when they weren't slaughtering innocents? Or did he actually believe in the *Imago Dei*, the ineffable metaphysical value of all human life?

It was a familiar treadmill. He would not resolve it tonight, not by another session of midnight introspection. Best to move on. Thirteen down, Latin phrase, blank *mori*. Must be *memento,* and that would work with the next word across.

Dawn came sooner than he expected, and he lay back down to sleep, if sleep would come.

Langer was just settling in behind his desk when Triple-A came into his office. He looked up from reading the third-watch report and stared at her.

"They need you down at Hotel Island," she said. "There's been a murder."

He closed his eyes. He should've been on it sooner. Should've gone through that place like a wrecking ball. Now someone was dead... His eyes snapped open. Triple-A was still there.

"Who?" he asked. "Any ID on the victim?"

"Nope. Just a male victim, off the roof. No further details."

Sending an amateur undercover: that was dangerous. He shouldn't have done it. He could've taken the place apart without deputizing Vowel. And now he would get to preside over the murder scene, to burn it into his memory so that he would never do it again. Experience is such a cruel teacher.

He would have the entire trip down to Ilwaco to decide if he officially, for the record, knew that O had gotten a job as a steward. And to decide whether to identify the body on site, or to stall until the ME had O on a table. If O had discovered anything at all, revealing the undercover operation too soon might ruin results that O had died for. And waiting too late – Well, but did he even know that O had managed to get anything useful?

He wondered if he should call those two detectives from down in Salinas, but he dismissed that thought with prejudice. He didn't need Hollywood up here; there was enough drama without it.

Thirty-five minutes later, he pulled his cruiser into the circle in front of the lobby. A valet waved him towards the adjacent loading dock, so Langer followed the directions and parked next to a small man in a black suit, who stood as if waiting for him.

"Sheriff," said Kurt Foulard, as soon as the car door opened, "This is just, it's just completely unacceptable."

Langer pulled himself to his full height and gave the short man a blank look. He was thinking that the diminutive GM was mighty brave for so small a person. Foulard took half a step back but kept up the verbal assault.

"This can't go on. Something has to be done."

"About people dying in this hotel? You're right, something has to be done. And I'm doing it."

"Look, can you be more discreet this time? The hotel has a reputation. A great reputation."

Langer lowered his eyelids halfway and pushed past the little man, moving to the rear of the car. He took a Gladstone bag from his trunk. "Where's the body?"

Foulard raised his arm and snapped his fingers. A valet trotted over to them. "Show the sheriff the scene. Go around the back way." Foulard stalked into the kitchen, leaving Langer with the valet. Langer glanced at the valet's nametag, which read Micah.

"If you'll follow me," said Micah, indicating a path beside the loading dock. Micah led Langer down a set of steps, along a sidewalk, past the rear of the kitchen. Langer noted a small herb garden. His eyes automatically scanned for those certain herbs that shouldn't be there. His quick glance didn't raise any red flags.

The trail wove between a couple of sheds, discreetly hidden from public view by trellises and vines, then sharply down the rocky hillside. At last, the path ended, leaving Langer and Micah on a rocky shore several stories below the immense windows of the restaurant. A deputy had already covered the body, and was photographing small jetsam nearby.

"What've we got?" asked Langer, as Micah turned and jogged back up the trail.

"Went off the roof sometime in the night. Holding a bottle of wine at the time. Struck one ledge, there…" The deputy pointed back up the cliff, where a narrow sloping ridge had been disturbed. "Rebounded here. Probably dead after hitting the ledge."

"Suicide, maybe?"

"Not likely," said the deputy. "There are defensive wounds on the palms and forearms. Someone attacked him with a kitchen knife or something like it."

"He didn't get those in the fall?"

"Hard to see how," said the deputy. "And he certainly didn't get stabbed in the chest on his way down."

Langer drew a deep breath and sighed. "Any ID?"

"Jackson Johns. Works here. We found his wallet, plus the General Manager recognized him."

Langer quickly looked down at the dead body, then back at the deputy. "The sommelier? You're sure?"

"Was he? Well, that explains the wine bottle." The deputy pointed to shattered fragments of a wine bottle.

"Anything else unusual?"

"Not by comparison."

"When did it happen?"

"Near as we can figure, between midnight and six AM. Night cleaners were finishing up in the restaurant, and one of them saw him down here. Ilwaco dispatch couldn't raise any of their officers, and referred it over to us around quarter to seven. Been here since."

"Take your time. Get as much information as you can."

"Once the tide comes in, it's all over," said the Deputy. "But I'll get what I can before that. Morgue will have someone out for the body in about twenty or thirty minutes."

Langer looked up the cliff. The small ledge was maybe twenty feet above the shore. It tapered outwards, towards the sea. There was a patch of vegetation knocked loose and dangling over the edge. Above the ledge, the huge rocks formed an irregular cliff, with the edge just below huge glass windows that leaned out over the uneven shore.

If it had happened earlier, during dinner, Langer would have had more witnesses than he could possibly use. As it was, he'd be lucky to find anyone who had seen anything. The motive, at least, was clear. Johns had reported embezzlement, and suddenly he took a short flight off of a tall roof. No rocket science there.

"You've been up on the roof?"

"I sent somebody. I wanted to get done here before the tide came in. No drag marks, no real signs of a struggle, but it's a gravel roof, so you can't really tell." He shrugged. "No artifacts of note. There was a small puddle that might have been vinegar."

"You took a sample, I hope. How do you get out onto the roof from here?"

"The stairwell by the kitchen? Well, from the top landing there's a staircase up to a kind of a storage room. Has windows all around; you can see it from the circle. They call it the cupola room.

"I guess it was for HVAC parts at one time. Looks like this guy turned it into a kind of an office or a tasting room. Sort of cozy up there. He had a nice chair and a rug."

"It has a door to the roof?"

"A casement window, very slight step up over the sill, but it might as well be a door. The latch was open and the window was ajar. So he could've gone up there alone, maybe. Maybe not."

"You got pictures of that room and the roof and the whole deal, right? Looked for anything unusual?"

"Yeah. Looked like a comfy spot up there. Even a bookshelf and some books, mostly about grapes. I guess when it's a slow night, you need a place to wait until someone wants a special wine."

Langer turned back to the crime scene. The deputy was snapping pictures of the broken wine bottle. Langer made his way back up to his car.

Kurt Foulard sat at his desk, fuming. Last year, it was his predecessor, Titus Bretz, dying during the Great Chefs of Today festival. To make matters worse, Titus was followed by his widow a couple days later. As if Titus dying on him wasn't bad enough. He wondered if Rustoff were in the hotel. He needed to shout at someone.

He looked out the picture window that formed one wall of his office, overlooking the herb garden. If he stood in the right place, he could see the ocean through a stand of pine trees.

While he watched, Sheriff Langer trudged up the hill, past the herb garden, and out of sight near the loading dock. Langer, the neat-and-careful law-and-order type. Plodding along, with no imagination at all. If he had any clue what Kurt and Oleg were up to … well, it was a good thing Langer was clueless.

Langer was no match for him, decided Foulard. Last year, Langer never got within a hundred miles of knowing what was really going on here. He was too focused on the murders to see anything else. Kurt grinned at the idea of his own superiority. He was the grandmaster here, and there was no way that anyone could ever outsmart him.

The intercom buzzed. "Mister Foulard, I have someone here for you," said Demetria, his secretary.

"Who is it?" he snapped, softening his tone at just the last second. He didn't want Demetria mad at him. She still thought he had divorced Vanity so that he could marry her.

"Someone from Littoral Properties," replied Demetria. He could almost hear her shrug her shoulders.

No one at the home office had called to say that they were coming out to Washington, so this caught him by surprise. He couldn't imagine what would have gotten someone in Chicago to jump onto a plane … Well, it might be that they were out on the Coast about something else; maybe a new acquisition?

That thought was interesting. Kurt liked the idea of getting his fingers into yet another pie. Perhaps Littoral was taking over another resort: Of course they'd need his help. No one else knew the hotel business the way that he did. And of course, setting up a hotel the right way enabled one to set it up for one's own best interests. There might be a huge opportunity.

Maybe he could set up a couple new income streams… Well, best not to get the horse before the cart when you make him drink. Chickens and hatchets, all that.

Kurt pulled himself to full height, even though his full height wasn't very impressive. He walked over to the door and pulled it open, managing a smile that was intended show to mild curiosity, despite the grossly uncivilized interruption to vital hotel business.

A woman stood there. She wore a dark green pantsuit. She was not very tall, though taller than Kurt, and she might perhaps have been a few points on the wrong side of the body mass index. She smiled a professional smile and extended a hand. "Melanie Nador," she said. "May I come in?"

He stood aside as she entered, then closed the door behind her. She moved near the window. "I love your view," she said.

"Yes, well," he said, casually taking his place behind his desk, as if he were jaded to such mundane displays. "It's the general manager's privilege, I suppose. How can I help you?"

"I'm your new Rooms Division Manager. To fill the position formerly held by Leon Rothenberg?"

He grimaced. How did Demetria get this one so very wrong? This wasn't someone from corporate; it was a job applicant. He'd have to have harsh words with her about letting a job applicant get access to him. And then, of course, buy her dinner to stay in her good graces.

In the meantime, he was amazed at the cheek of this woman. Coming straight into the general manager's office, instead of going through HR? Unthinkable. And she probably hadn't even brought a resume; she likely presumed that speaking to the GM was all it would take to settle things.

That alone, that utter unawareness of how hotels ran, would disqualify her, even if they had actually intended to fill the position. Why, having the nerve to do this; it was simply rude. It was like a slap in the face.

"We're not actually planning to fill that position." He said it with an air of finality, as if to suggest that this woman, no matter what she had heard, was committing a horrible business *faux pas*.

"Whether you were planning to or not, you have."

Kurt couldn't decide if she were trying to impress him with her nerve, or if she simply didn't understand him. Was she hoping he'd be intrigued by her boldness? Or maybe impressed with her determination?

"I'm afraid that I don't understand," he said, after a moment.

She opened a leather-bound portfolio and produced a letter. "You should have received this in the mail last week?" she asked.

The paper seemed oddly familiar. He lifted the stack of papers on the right side of his desk and quickly thumbed through them.

Most of them were memos, a few were letters. About an inch down, there it was.

He skimmed the letter, mumbling words at random as he did. "Bearer of this letter, Melanie Nador, your new Rooms Division Manager... transition..." He looked up. "It seems as if I have no choice in the matter."

"You really don't. I'm with Gyannt Resorts, and Littoral Properties kindly agreed to help us prepare for the transition."

"You're the advance man."

"I'm an advance person," she corrected. "I'm here to make sure we understand the operation of the hotel and any local business practices, so that the cut-over will be as smooth and efficient as possible."

"Well, of course we wish to continue to work with the ownership group. We were planning for a smooth transition period, but we assumed that Littoral Properties would help all the way through. And the transition isn't for months. This is simply, well, premature. Very premature!"

Melanie smiled, reading between the lines. It was always like this in management group cutovers. The old management company – Littoral Properties, in this case – always wanted to extend things, and to charge for as many managers as possible, for as long as possible. She expected a bit of file-hiding and some disputes over whether the new group would have enough expertise to maintain the prestige of the hotel. The usual drama.

Her first course of action would be to secure the hotel's working files, of course: the budgets, the financials, the ledgers, the trial ledgers, and all the email accounts of the accounting staff. But she would do that quietly, behind the scenes, before Kurt and his cronies had a chance to doctor them up or to hide them.

Surprise was her ally. It was a very powerful tool, and she wielded it well. She would let them think she was blind. Distraction, misdirection; she would pretend not to notice a few subtle gestures here or there ... and then she would yank the rug out from under them. Managers who lied to Melanie always regretted it.

"Yes, of course," said Melanie, smiling a crocodilian grin. "And I'm really the wrong person to ask about that. I'm just the manager who drew the short end of the straw. So I'm the advance person. And even after the cutover, they're going to want someone from Littoral to stay on for a while as a point of contact for the hotel staff. Naturally, you'll choose that person."

"Right. I assumed we'd negotiate all that…"

"Again, wrong person to ask. I just work here. So to speak."

"So," said Kurt, feeling a slight throb in his temples. "When do you start?" He wondered if there were time to run through the books with Celia, the Assistant Controller, to make sure that the hidden enterprises were well-concealed.

"Today," she replied. "I took the liberty of reserving a room for myself. It's the smallish suite on the cliff side, under the Ocean meeting room."

"Not that one. It rents for three hundred a night, even in the off-season," protested Kurt. "We have rooms near the pool area that we normally use for staff…"

"This is not the normal situation. You'll want to read that letter again, Kurt. It's all been arranged, and besides, I've moved in. I'll just go up and see my office."

She rose, extended her fingers to be pinched between his, and left the room. Kurt pinched the bridge of his nose and sighed. It was happening too fast. The throbbing in his temple spread across his forehead. It was like a slap in the face.

He reached for the phone.

Becka and Arinae stood in the dining room, looking down at the crime scene far below.

"Do you think he jumped?" asked Becka.

"I know that guy," said Arinae. "He's the head sommelier."

"The wine guy? Jack, or John?"

"Yeah. Jackson Johns. And that looks like a wine bottle down there. The thing that the deputy is putting into a bag."

"Parts of a wine bottle, at least."

"Can you imagine?"

"I've never worked in a hotel where somebody died," said Becka. "Well, you know, except that murder last year. But that was different." She wasn't sure how it was different, but she was certain that it was, possibly because the passage of time had tarnished its bright edges.

"I've never worked in a hotel before, period," said Arinae. "So I wouldn't know."

"This doesn't normally happen."

"I hope not."

"Are you new in the area?"

"No, I, uh, used to live further north. Came down here for the work, you know."

"I used to work here once before. Then I got married and moved to Dallas. That was a mistake."

"What's Dallas like?"

"Hot. Too hot, too often, for too long."

"I bet it doesn't rain all the time, like here."

"This isn't too bad. You start to miss the rain after a while."

"You just moved back?"

"Yeah, left my ex-husband there. Weird thing is, I met him here. He came for a food festival we did last Spring."

"Staying with family?"

"Got a small place by Long Beach. But it's three bedrooms and a little pricey."

"Need a roommate? I've been staying with friends, and they're starting to hint they want their couch back."

Becka turned to look Rina in the eye, her face serious. "Yeah, I dunno. My daughter's only three, so it's kind of..."

"Look, I don't do drugs or anything. I don't have a boyfriend. I just, it's just me. I don't snore, and I know how to use a vacuum cleaner. And I do my own dishes."

"Tell you what," said Becka. "Let me think about it. You here all night?"

"Yeah. I got a split shift; after lunch I'm off for a while, but I'll be back at three to set up for dinner."

"I'm off at five. I'll stop by before I leave and let you know." Becka turned and strolled out of the dining room, towards the front desk. Arinae watched her for a moment, then turned back to the scene on the rocks below.

It would be good to get a real place, but then again, if it didn't work out, it didn't work out. Like the guy who brought her down here from South Bend. That didn't work out either, but it was an improvement over living with her bat-crazy mother.

Technically, the friends whose couches she was surfing were all his friends. He was off somewhere looking for something. Telluride, maybe, or Vail, or some kind of a place where he just could be a ski bum and tell stories about deep powder. So, a real place, even just a real room, would be a step towards truly making her own way.

She had overheard the waiters talking about a room at the top of the stairs, where Jackson used to go take naps on the slow nights. Maybe they'd let her put a cot up there.

Nah, a store room for naps was one thing, especially for someone on salary whose income was tied to his sales. Her, a waiter, living in a storeroom; that was something else. She'd get into trouble for sure.

She sighed and got busy setting tables.

Steve Sauer was in early. Too early, by far. His shift ended at one AM, normally, and sometimes two, when there were problems. Last night, it was two-thirty. There hadn't been any big issues, but the sum of several small issues made it a long evening.

A cash drawer was short, and the front desk clerk was frantic. And rightly so. Ninety dollars isn't a huge sum, unless it comes out of your pocket, when you're only making a hundred-ten a night. Then, it's a huge deal.

Steve spent a good twenty minutes recounting the drawer. When a drawer is off by a multiple of nine, the error is almost always two transposed digits. Finding the problem resolved the issue, but it took time.

While that was going on, there had been a report of bedbugs. The bedbugs turned out to be apple seeds, which look remarkably like bedbugs from a distance. Even though it was the guest's own snacking that caused the problem, Steve took twenty dollars off the room rate for good will.

There was the tub overflow in three-oh-four that spilled into two-oh-four. There was the child reported ill, but don't call an ambulance, oh wait, it's just gas, never mind. There was a slightly drunk guest in the bar.

There was the server who broke a glass and cut himself. There was the guest concerned about another guest's fireplace smoke. And so it had gone, all night long, until Steve finally got to finish his own work. His own work consisted of reports, mostly, and a bit of light bookkeeping for the night shift at the desk.

In the end, he hadn't gotten home until nearly three.

The result of the late night was a version of Steve who, at nine-thirty in the morning, looked less than fully prepared for the day ahead. He would barely have time after this meeting to go home before he was needed back at the hotel again for the night shift.

But the all-important meetings will not be delayed. Time, tide, and reports on the current financial status of the hotel will wait for no one. Not even for the night manager.

Oleg Rustoff was waiting in the loading dock when the dry cleaner arrived. As the driver backed up to the dock and stopped, Rustoff came over to the driver's window.

"Listen," he said, "There's a new Rooms Division Manager. So you keep bringing the invoices and the deliveries to me, but at the food and beverage office, by the tasting room. Stay away from the front office. Clear?"

"This new rooms manager ..."

"Doesn't know the score. Stay away from her. Clear?"

"But you can still handle things, right?"

"We'll talk to Louis about the long term. But for now, you talk to me and only me. Nobody but me. Are we clear?"

The driver nodded. Rustoff nodded back, straightened up, and walked towards the circle in front of the lobby, smoothing his jacket over his belly.

The dry cleaner watched him walk away, and started unloading the racks of clean clothes. New managers who didn't know about the arrangement. That would change things.

Orin Kaltwasser was late. He was normally in the hotel by nine, at the latest. He would usually step out around one, and was usually back by six to work until ten or eleven that evening. He didn't need to be in the hotel for all of those hours. He had set up a system that worked very well, with people whom he trusted.

Trust might be too strong a word. The system worked well with people upon whom he relied. That was more accurate. He knew that each of his subordinates would play their role appropriately, and that his standards would be upheld. The key to the success of a restaurant is always in the standards, after all. Still, he kept long hours. He didn't know exactly why. But he did.

Today, with just minutes until ten o'clock, and the dreaded weekly management meeting, he would need to rush. He would pass quickly through the kitchen, mainly to show the flag. He would retrieve his notes from his office, and then be seen in the café for a moment before speeding to the meeting.

But he came to a stop in the kitchen.

Something was off. Cooks and prep staff who were normally moving energetically, making the kitchen ready for lunch, were instead gathered in clusters of two and three, chattering among themselves. Four of the cooks were standing with the daytime sous-chef, Bruce.

Bruce Stanley was a large man, six-five and three hundred. His face was shaved smooth, but the chef knew that under the tall chef's hat, there was a coiled pony-tail hidden from view. So long as it stayed hidden, Orin was okay with it. As Orin approached, the cooks turned and resumed their duties.

"What's going on?" asked Orin.

"It's Jackson," said Bruce. "He went off the roof last night."

Off the roof. That could be a metaphor, Orin supposed. Hit the ceiling, went off the roof, the roof is on fire, whatever the newest phrase was. Surely he didn't … No, of course not. Because Jackson – it was unthinkable.

"He – what happened?"

"Went off the roof. Jumped. Holding a bottle of Xino Chymo, if you can believe that."

"Where did you hear this?" asked Orin, his eyes roving the kitchen, his mind willing them to find Jackson Johns, willing it to be a rumor, or a joke.

"It's all over the hotel. Night cleaners spotted the body. Sheriff's still down there, collecting evidence."

The look on Orin's face expressed his disbelief far better than words. Bruce sighed. He touched Orin's elbow and nodded towards the dining room, leading the chef out to the window, where they peered down at the scene. The officers had gone, but the yellow plastic tape remained, around rocks that were slowly submerging in the rising tide.

The scene was vanishing, but the meaning remained.

"Is he…"

"Dead," said Bruce. "Not a great way to go."

"Why?" asked Orin. Bruce shrugged.

"Look, you've got the meeting. I'll get the team back on track. We'll call in Javier to cover tonight."

Orin, still slightly stunned, nodded and made his way to his office, where he took the stack of papers on the desk and walked out the one-way door into the lobby.

Kurt rapped on the table with his knuckles, drawing the managers away from their side conversations. Chairs were pulled in, heads turned towards the end of the table, and silence fell.

If only it were always this easy to get their attention, he thought. *Maybe throwing someone off the roof should become a weekly thing.*

"Let's get down to business," he said. "We've got a couple of big things to talk about. First of all, you will have heard that Jackson Johns had an unfortunate accident this morning.

"We can't prevent the staff from talking about it, but we need to discourage, as much as possible, the spreading of the speculation and gossip. Oleg, we'll need to arrange a memorial of some sort. Something in one of the small meeting rooms, like this one, just for staff and managers. Let 'em get it out of their system."

"It might take longer," said Melanie, at Kurt's left side. "We may want to bring on grief counselors, and have HR send out flyers about stress relief and suicide prevention."

"Excuse me," said Steve. "Jackson committed suicide?"

"It's too early to say," said Kurt, glaring at Melanie. "The police are still looking into Jackson's death. It appears to be self-inflicted. But we don't want to start anything."

"Even if we don't want to say that it was suicide," said Melanie, "It's going to take longer than one memorial meeting for the staff to process their grief."

"My father died last year," snapped Kurt. "I grieved for three days. Then I got over it. That's how long grief takes: Three days."

"So, what exactly did happen?" said Orin. "I'm just now finding out about this."

"He got dr—"

"He seems to have been on the roof," said Oleg, cutting off whatever Kurt was about to say. "And he had a bottle of wine with him. He and the bottle went off the roof. That's all we know for now. The police are still investigating it. When we know more, we'll tell you. But for now, we want to keep rumors under control."

Oleg sent a stern gaze around the room, saying, without words, that the subject was closed. His look, despite his painful smile, was far more effective than Kurt's words.

"On a more pleasant note," said Kurt, "We are pleased to announce the arrival of the new Rooms Division Manager, Melanie Nador. She will be settling into her office as soon as Oleg can get his things moved out of it."

Oleg almost smiled at the term, "Pleasant." It most certainly was not pleasant, and Kurt was not at all pleased to announce Melanie. No one on the executive committee would be pleased by this development.

"Melanie," continued Kurt, "Why don't you tell us a little about yourself?"

"Gladly," she said, with a courteous smile. "I was raised in Omaha, began my career as a bar server during college, and moved to Minneapolis with my first husband, where we worked together at the Gyannt Carlisle. From there, I served as a Rooms Manager in Miami. Three years in Cayman Brac, Director of Operations at the newly-opened Gyannt Atlantic, and for the last seven years, I've been working out of the Gyannt Corporation home offices in Nashville."

"What brings you to the Inn at River Columbia?" asked Oleg, with a crocodile smile. "After Nashville…" He left it hanging, but the meaning was clear: *After Nashville, a backwater resort was a step down, and a demotion.* That would put her into her place.

"It's a special project," she replied, looking equally crocodilian. "I'll be leading the transition to Gyannt Resorts Management."

She watched with amusement as glances sped round the room. She tried to make note of which eyes met for significant seconds, but it was all too fast. Beneath the placid corporate veneer, panic was spreading through the meeting, compounding with each subtle turn of the eyes.

That was good. Something was wrong here, and she would find it out. And the more rattled these people were, the easier her job would become. Panic causes mistakes. One or more of these very rattled managers would say something he shouldn't, or would do something she shouldn't, and just like that, Melanie would have them. She kept a perfectly calm face as she sat down.

But on the inside, she was grinning from ear to ear.

Chapter Six

O CAME IN EARLY. It was only three or so, but he needed to get out of his loft, and work was the only other place to go. He didn't feel like driving all the way back up to his place in South Bend, only to come back again for his next shift.

There was something different about the rhythm of the kitchen, but he couldn't put his finger on it. He didn't bother himself with it. If something important were going on, he'd hear about it soon enough.

He went down to the basement, where the break area nestled under the café patio. It was just outside the official staff lunch room, a desolate little space next to the locker rooms.

The outdoor break area consisted of a couple of park-style wooden tables with built in benches, screened from the pool deck by redwood lattices overgrown with vines. The general ambiance was subdued light, or else muted darkness.

He got a caffeinated soda from the soda machine and seated himself on one of the benches to work some crossword puzzles. Arinae was standing at the other end of the break area, staring blankly towards the pool through one of the holes in the lattice. She held a cigarette between her fingers, but she seemed to have forgotten it, and the ash was moving perilously close to her skin.

To sleep, blank to dream. That would be *perchance*. Mexican holiday, with the letters already there, would have to be *Dia de los Muertos*. Who is buried in Grant's Tomb? The expected answer would be *Grant*, but actually it's no one: President and Mrs. Grant are entombed there. Still, it fit the necessary letters. Kind of a morbid theme in the crosswords, it seemed.

"Oh, hey, Al," said Arinae, spotting him at last.

He looked up. "Hey," he said, in a friendly tone, and started to lower his eyes back to the crossword.

"Hear about Jackson?"

"Um, no." About Jackson… He raised his eyes, while trying to keep any interest from showing in his face. Jackson could have done any number of things: made a big scene in the restaurant, gotten fired, resigned, come to work drunk…

"He jumped off the roof."

"He did what?"

"Or maybe he was pushed. No one knows. It happened sometime last night."

"What, how, I mean, do they know what happened?" he asked, pushing the crossword aside.

"Nobody knows for sure, but apparently he took a bottle of Xino Chymo, drank it on the roof – they found the cork up there – and then he jumped, bottle and all."

"Xino Chymo?"

"Yeah, it's real pricey stuff. Like five grand a bottle, can you believe that?" She suddenly became aware of the cigarette and stubbed it out against a redwood slat before walking over to his table. "I guess if you're gonna go, price doesn't matter, but…" She shrugged and sat down across from him. "Kinda gives you the creeps, you know? When somebody you know does something like that, right? Suicide? "

"It wasn't suicide," he said.

"What? How do you know?"

O caught himself. He knew that it wasn't suicide because he knew that Johns wouldn't have chosen Trocken Weider Gobi for his last taste of wine. And that's what would have been in the Chymo bottle, if Johns' story were true. But he shouldn't have blurted it out.

"I mean, I'm sure he wouldn't, just, you know, without some kind of warning..." He shrugged and tried to look stupid, which is not easy for someone who isn't.

"Well, what else could it be? You don't think..." She mouthed the word "murder" as if it were too horrible to say out loud.

"What do I know?" he asked. "I'm just a dishwasher."

"Yeah, but... no, that's... I mean, why would someone kill him? He was a really nice guy. I mean, genuinely nice. He always tipped us, you know, when he made good commissions on his sales. And he was real, not just like when people are nice because you're a girl, you know?"

"I'm afraid I don't," said O.

Arinae blushed a little. "Anyway, yeah, no one would kill him. Not Jackson."

O frowned. He'd need to call Langer and report this.

"The sheriff was out there earlier," continued Arinae. "I was watching it from the big windows with Becka, that one woman that works at front desk. She said she had never worked in a hotel where somebody died. Well, except for a murder here last year."

Okay, maybe O wouldn't need to call Langer. But this wasn't the sort of thing he had signed on for. It was supposed to be about gaining trust and keeping an eye on the kitchen – watching Johns work, seeing who, if anyone, tampered with the wines.

He used his thumb and forefinger to stroke his upper lip, where his mustache used to be.

"You used to have a mustache, didn't you?" she asked.

"How did you know?"

"You did that thing, where you stroke the mustache. My dad used to do that." She shook her head. "Man, it's weird. You don't think about how somebody's here one day, and then... just like that." She shivered, even though it wasn't cold.

He nodded his head as if he, too, were pondering the fragility of life, but he was actually wondering what this meant in more immediate terms. If they caught Johns – if they knew he had talked – then it could be dangerous for O as well. One murder or ten murders; the penalty is the same: Life without parole.

Had Johns spotted him? Did Johns know that O was here, undercover, and if so, did he tell someone before he tried to fly? If the answers were "yes," then this was a good time to disappear.

But if O were to just run away… Suddenly vanishing right after the murder would draw attention to himself. So it might be better to stay put for a while. Yes. He would stay put, keep his mouth shut and his ears open. And after it was old news – or at least not the big blaring headline – he would quietly quit and go back up to South Bend. Justice would take its course, with or without him.

"What do you know about Rina?" asked Becka.

Steve looked up from the front desk PC. "Who… the new waiter in the restaurant?"

"Yeah. Kind of thin, kind of quiet, but really intense when she talks to you?"

"Right, yeah. What about her?"

"She was asking if I wanted to share my apartment."

Steve shrugged and turned back to the screen. "I dunno, I guess it might work. You'd have to talk to her, you know, get some references and stuff."

"Yeah. She seems okay, but I'm trying to be careful with my daughter. I don't want druggies around or anything."

"She doesn't strike me as a user." Steve looked back down at the screen. "I mean, you can't always tell. But I don't think she is."

"Yeah. I guess I'll just talk to her and see. So isn't that weird, about Jackson?"

Steve nodded sadly, then turned back to his work. Or rather, he turned back to the work he did to keep himself busy when he had downtime during the shift.

As a manager, he was non-exempt, and was paid by the work he accomplished rather than the hours he worked. But since his assignments included observing and guiding the night-time hourly staff, he couldn't leave early. It was the worst of both worlds.

The net result was time that had to be killed in some subtle and yet defensible way. Sometimes, when the desk was slow, he'd take a long walk around the island, ostensibly to see that everything was in order and that the wildlife was keeping to itself, but with the actual goal of being near enough to fix any catastrophes while far enough not to overhear the telephone operator calling his girlfriend.

He sometimes invented projects for himself, and his current make-work project was a small computer program that he hoped would automate the daily reports. By drawing data from the actual deposits, it would calculate past and future average daily rates and occupancy figures. These would go into graphs on the front page of a GUI that he designed himself.

He told himself that he was doing this for the good of the hotel, and that once it was working well, he'd take it to Oleg and Kurt to get their sign off on the project. Maybe the entire thing would become standard for Littoral Properties as a whole.

In actual fact, Steve simply was teaching himself the SQL database language, while getting practice in Visual Basic for Applications. It really didn't matter if he created something useful or not, so long as he learned and it killed time.

And if that experience, and the skills he picked up on this pet project … well, if he happened to get a better job as a result of this little endeavor, that wouldn't be his fault. After all, it was for the good of the hotel. It would automate the box scores.

He ran a report, but once again, it didn't come out right. The margins were offset to the left by about an inch from where he wanted them, so the edge of the paper cut off the first character of each line, rendering the report unreadable.

And the sums were simply wrong. They weren't off by an incredible amount, but they were clearly not correct. He guessed that they might be about four times higher than they should be.

He sighed. He'd need to take a deep dive and get back into the code. It ought to be a simple formula: Take the gross revenue, divide by the number of days, and there's your Average Daily Rate. Take the number of possible room-nights, divide by the actual rooms sold, and shazam: Your average occupancy.

But it was coming out wrong. Obviously, somewhere in his code, one of the instructions he had written was taking the wrong data and adding it into the wrong column. There was no way to find it but going through the source code line by line.

Good thing he had all night to get it done.

"So, where's O today?" asked Triple-A, smiling brightly at the assembled cold-case team. She was holding a small casserole dish, covered in foil.

"Sheriff said he called in, maybe a bit of a cold." Millie shrugged, as if she couldn't care less. Her facial expression suggested that she wasn't upset at his absence. "We'll email the minutes to him."

Shelley looked up from her knitting and peered over her readers at Aiden's covered dish. "What have you got there, Dear?" she asked.

Triple-A put the casserole dish on the table with an audible clunk. "I baked some cookies for the Auxiliary," she said. "Hope you enjoy them." She omitted the smile that such a gesture called for, and instead showed a trace of disappointment.

Shelley peered under the foil. "Oh, they look lovely," she remarked, to Triple-A's retreating back.

O made his way into the kitchen and approached the dishwasher. The steward on duty, a big red-haired guy with a goofy expression and thick glasses, was dumping the final rinse tank, in preparation for refilling it with fresh water. Steam rose from the drain sinks as the water spilled out into them. The drain sink under the primary wash tank had also just been dumped, as the plastic strainer in that drain sink testified.

The steward on duty looked at the drain sink strainer, filled with plastic coffee stirrers and bits of foil, along with one jumbo shrimp and a couple corks. He took off his huge rubber gloves before reaching down to flip the strainer over. He had to thump it on the bottom of the drain sink a couple times before the debris all vanished down into the two-inch pipe below.

Proud of his expert effort, he flipped the strainer upright and put the gloves on again. Then he glanced behind him and saw O.

"Hey, Al. In early, huh?" he said.

"Hey, Mac. Couldn't sleep. Everything goin' okay?"

The large steward shrugged and turned his round face towards O. "Yeah, 'cept for Jackson. You heard?"

"Yeah. Hey, are we supposed to turn over the strainers like that? Doesn't it make the drains clog?"

Mac shrugged again. "Makes it go away," he said, in what might have been an argument, or perhaps a simple statement of fact. O decided not to pursue the matter.

"Reminds me of that animated movie," he quipped. *"How to Drain your Dragon."*

Mac stared at him blankly. "How to…"

"Yeah, silly joke. Never mind."

Mac turned back towards the dishwasher and started re-filling the tank, but the confused look stayed on his face. O decided not to make any more jokes with Mac. Or maybe he just shouldn't make any more jokes at all.

Arinae walked through the dining room, carefully picking up wineglasses and polishing them with a soft cloth and a gentle grip. The gentle grip was what made the difference between a glass that sparkled and a bloody handful of broken glass. Apparently something like that happened at the GCOT festival once, because every manager in the kitchen went on and on about the gentle grip when polishing glasses.

They were supposed to wear special white cloth gloves, as if the single layer of super-fine fabric would actually do anything for broken glass. But that was the rule.

She had heard a lot of rumors about the annual GCOT festivals, and she wasn't sure whether to be excited about them, or a little frightened. They sounded very intense. She had also heard about the GCOT festival last year, where two people had died. Not from broken glass, of course. But still, best to be careful.

She looked at the huge windows, angled out over the rocks below, looking down on the rapid River Columbia and the immense ocean beyond. Normally she found the view intimidating because the world beyond that window was just so incredibly huge.

Tonight it was doubly intimidating, because just down there, on those rocks… of course, the body was gone by now. Even the crime tape had been taken down. She thought about later on, when the night would be over, and she didn't have to look down at that scene any more. And then what?

She would go home – or to the borrowed couch that wasn't really hers – and she would lay in the dark thinking about it. About Jackson Johns, dead down there on those rocks. Maybe a suicide, and maybe (if Al was right) a murder victim. But either way, not coming back. Just gone. Over. Done.

Times like this, when the harsh, cruel nature of life broke into the careful dream, the story that we tell ourselves – those were the times when Rina felt alone. Growing up, her silly name had made it tough to make friends, and she really didn't have a truly close relationship with anyone to this day. She'd have liked to talk about Jackson with someone, with anyone, if she only had someone to talk with.

She didn't exactly miss her ex-boyfriend, who was out partying in Telluride, but on the other hand, it would've been nice to have someone she could talk to about it. Someone who'd understand; someone who knew her and would get why the sudden death of a coworker, even one she barely knew, was making her feel like this. Even that jerk of an ex-boyfriend would've been nice to have around. Anyone would do.

Maybe she could talk it through with that dishwasher guy. He seemed like he might be a good listener. And he hadn't stared at her or made her feel creepy, so he probably wouldn't get the wrong idea about it. Kinda friendly, but mostly detached.

Becka Corwallis, who had been Becka Landreaux last year, and Becka Smithson four years ago, stood at the front desk and thought about Jackson Johns. She hadn't known him well. He seemed like a nice enough guy, maybe a drunk – he had those tell-tale veins on the side of his nose – but a very polite, friendly, and well-mannered man, nonetheless.

And without any warning, he was gone, just like that. It was jarring, but it was just as jarring that life went on without him. Did he even matter? Had he really even been here? The restaurant went on, the hotel went on. In a few days, he would just be someone who, sadly, had worked here. And had died here.

And then a guest came in, so Becka applied her professional smile, and laid aside Jackson's memory for a more convenient time.

"And where is O this time?" asked Millie. "We postponed this meeting so we could work around his schedule."

Shelley looked up from her knitting. "Maybe he's sick."

"That's an understatement. There's something very wrong with that man."

"I meant ill. You know, the flu or something."

"Oh. Maybe."

"We could possibly have a patrol car swing by his place, make sure he's okay."

"I guess we could ask the sheriff."

"Or possibly Triple-A. She's on the radio with them."

Millie made a face. "I'll ask the sheriff."

"Did Diane have anything new to say about Arinae?"

"Just that it's just like the sheriff to give this case to the lost cause squad. She was very concerned that he didn't have the time for it himself. Just another lost cause."

"Lost causes?" Shelley grimaced. "Well, that hardly seems fair. We've closed, what, three cases last year?"

"Four if you count the Gardner case. But that was…"

"Petty theft is still a crime."

"They would have figured it out anyway. It was kind of obvious when you think about it."

"But they never bothered to think about it. That's how we got the case." She perled three stitches.

"I told Diane that O was looking at this as a runaway case."

"I'm sure that went over well with her."

"She told me where O could go, and what he could do when he got there."

"Well, that's not very nice."

"Nice. I'm not sure that's in her vocabulary. But, look, she's just a mother who wants her little girl back home again."

"Maternity does not a mother make," said Shelley, knitting two and perling three. "That girl was never a daughter, just an accessory. Little more than a handbag or a bracelet."

"Like you're one to talk. Where are your precious children?"

"Don't get personal."

"You're gossiping about Diane, my best friend. Like that's not supposed to be personal?"

"This won't help us find Arinae."

"You dropped a stitch," gloated Millie. The two glared at each other for several minutes, until Shelley gathered her knitting and stormed out of the room.

Triple-A breezed in with a coffee cup in her hand. "Meeting over already?"

Millie ignored the question. "Has anyone heard from O?"

"I was going to send a car by his house, but the sheriff said not to bother. O's out of town for a few days."

"Coulda told us," snapped Millie. She scooped up her papers and marched out of the room.

"So, the bedroom with the one window, that would be yours, and there's just the one bathroom, so you'll have to deal with the bath toys and stuff like that. And Rachel always gets her bath at the same time, so you'll want to plan around it."

"No problem," said Rina. "I'll keep my towels in my room, and use my own shampoo and everything."

"Make sure you keep razors and anything sharp put up," said Becka. "I can't take any chances on Rachel finding them."

"You won't regret this," said Rina.

Becka took a deep breath and handed Rina the key. "I need to get my daughter from her sitter," she said.

Rina walked into her room, listening as Becka let herself out. The room was small, even as bedrooms go. But it was hers. The bare carpet, slightly worn where the traffic paths had been; the walls with faint smudges, the hand marks on the door jambs… it was her new home.

She'd need a futon, or something like it, to sleep on. She had seen one at Sally Ann's, and she could probably get it for cheap. She'd need a small table, and a dresser, and a lamp.

And curtains, even though the window looked out at a fenced-in side yard. Maybe she could get friends to help her bring in the big pieces. She wondered if there was any way she could wrestle a futon into the apartment by herself… but that was just impossible.

"Kurt," said Melanie, "We really need to talk about the safety training records. They are absolutely hopeless. If we had an OSHA audit tomorrow, we'd all get fired. The fines would be enormous! And I don't have to tell you the kind of scrutiny that the hotel would be under from that point forward."

"That's a personnel issue," snapped Kurt. "Let Marigold worry about it, and you concentrate on Rooms business."

"Kurt, you seem to forget who you're talking to," said Melanie, with a subtle edge to her voice. "When Gyannt takes over, the entire management team is responsible for having everything in order. All of us. You, me, Oleg, Celia, Marigold, everyone. So we need to have everything in proper order. Otherwise, there will be serious repercussions."

"Alright, alright, we'll talk about it in the staff meeting!" He scrawled a quick note onto a yellow sticky and pressed it to his desk. He'd give the sticky to Demetria, so she could type up notes about it, and maybe make herself useful for once.

"I'll be here late tonight, going through the training records, and, honestly, we've got to get a safety program established for the front office. There's nothing at all," continued Melanie.

"Yes, they could all get paper cuts." He sighed. "Do what you have to do." He hung up the phone. Why did she even bother to call him? She didn't work for him, and they both knew it. But even as the thought passed through his mind, he had the odd feeling that perhaps he did work for Melanie, in some odd roundabout way.

Melanie smiled. The safety records did need sorting; of course they did. They always do, and however thoroughly they're managed, they always will. When Gyannt came in, Gyannt would establish a new safety training program on day one, and blame any prior discrepancies on the management staff hired by Littoral Properties. That was simply standard procedure in any kind of hotel transfer or takeover. And since all but one of the current management staff would quit on day two – also standard operating procedure – there would be no one left to say otherwise.

But in the short term, Kurt would complain to Oleg, and Oleg was the real target of Melanie's barb. Kurt didn't have the brains for the things going on in this hotel; he clearly was a figurehead. So the obvious puppet-master was Oleg, and the key to Melanie's plan was deceiving him; convincing him that she was no threat at all. So long as he believed she was wasting her time protecting the hotel from OSHA fines and other legal details, he'd never guess her real target.

Her laptop had been specially designed for this. It had a SCSI-2 interface built into the motherboard. The SCSI-2 port looked like an old-fashioned parallel port, and the old-style printer cables would attach to it nicely, if one were so inclined. It wouldn't work as a printer port, but it looked like one.

The laptop and the other equipment were specially made for her by the head nerd in Nashville. It was carefully designed around the single special purpose of learning everything about a hotel that others did not wish for one to know.

Melanie used a special cable to attach a tape drive. It was old technology, thirty years or more out of date, but it allowed her to read the DAT tapes she had carefully copied from the backups in the computer room, beneath the hotel.

The reasoning behind her plan was simple: All the data, even the secret data, would have to be backed up every night. So the tapes were the obvious targets.

When the hotel's server was purchased, however many eons ago, it had used DAT as a backup device. There were stacks of tapes, each carefully dated, piled in the computer room. It appeared, from her cursory glance, that the tapes were reused every fourteen days, and that it took twelve tapes to back up the entire server.

The tapes, like the drive they serviced, were old and small. They had probably all been purchased when the server was new, and not replaced since. Newer larger tapes would have backed up the entire server in a single go. If the server had had USB interfaces, Melanie could have simply attached a 2-terabyte thumb drive and downloaded the entire server. But of course, that method would not get the files now in use, and it would retain the security structure built into the files.

The backup tapes, on the other hand, were recorded with system-level authority, bypassing minor issues of file ownership. Since her laptop could use an alternative operating system, breaking the files' ownership restrictions would be trivial, once she pulled them over onto the laptop.

"There is no security but physical," she muttered, as the first tape began to whir in the drive, sending its files to the laptop. She checked her watch. She had enough time, while the tape was running, to get a cup of coffee and to walk up the hill to Human Resources, maybe.

She closed and locked her door. The spring lock was the same old one that her predecessor had used. The deadbolt lock, however, she had carefully replaced herself one night, after everyone else had gone home, following the instructions given to her by Gyannt's head locksmith. The deadbolt featured an L-keyway, which no key blank in this hotel was likely to match, and had a hidden seventh pin as a safeguard against picking.

With that deadbolt in place, her office was as secure as she could make it without posting a guard, and while it would not withstand a dedicated attack by a skilled Bosnian lawyer, it would certainly withstand the casual interference of ordinary hotel staff. At least for a while.

The sun had gone down, and the wind had come up. She shrugged at the chill and stepped up her pace to fend off the cold.

HR was closed, of course. The HR staff was out at four, every night, without fail. That wouldn't matter. Her grand master key would let her into the office. The files she wanted would not be in the filing cabinets, and certainly not on the computers.

At the top of the hill, hidden by pine trees from the hotel proper, there was a two-story building with a sharp peaked roof. One quarter of the building was missing; that is, it had been designed in an ell-shape. The long side of the building had one continuous roof, all sloped downhill. The shorter side of the building, with the roof sloping towards the uphill side, was the laundry and housekeeping department.

Inside of the ell, the laundry and maintenance carts were bunched together, each connected to a charger and an extension cord that stretched back to the building itself. Overlooking this menagerie of electric carts, a balcony ran along the long side of the ell, providing access to the offices on the second floor.

The long roof covered the walkway above, and the demi-wall that ran the length of the walkway darkened the office doors and kept them mostly hidden from view. Now, in the late twilight, with bright flood lamps illuminating the electric carts, someone on the walkway would be virtually invisible.

Melanie had scouted this building earlier, under the guise of visiting the accounting office, on the second floor in the corner of the ell. Now, under the cover of falling darkness, she was ready to get to the bottom of things.

Marigold, the HR manager, was young enough to be able to use computers, but old enough to fear them. Marigold was of the generation who thought that accessing the internet for any reason, however innocent, was simply an invitation to be flooded with horrible pornographic images and dangerous viruses. She might use the computer in her office once in a while, under protest, but anything that she really wanted to "keep safe from hackers" would be on paper.

The only drawer that was locked was the bottom right desk drawer, and it used the stock lock that came with the desk. One key opened all desks of that model, and Melanie had that key.

Inside the drawer was a bonanza of personnel files. All of the executive team members were represented there, each in their own manila folder, each in their own dark green hanging file. Melanie filled her briefcase with the folders.

Copying them in HR would run up the counter on the copier, and that might suggest that personnel files had been copied. It would be much better for Melanie to go down to the housekeeping office, downstairs. The copier there was heavily used, and a few extra copies wouldn't stand out.

As she let herself out of HR, a chill wind swept along the breezeway, cutting through her clothes. It felt like a snow might be in the offing. She almost wished she'd worn a parka.

As she pondered the cold, Melanie noticed a dark figure stepping out of the maintenance shop, below her. She could only see the top of his head. She stood stock still, to be certain that she wouldn't be seen. The dark shadowy walkway rendered her almost invisible, and he probably had idea that she was there.

The hidden figure walked calmly and purposefully across the small yard, dodging through the electric carts and the large tangle of extension cords. He stopped at the back door of the laundry.

After a furtive look around, he stretched onto his toes and reached through the wooden flap on the door, which was intended to allow after-hours laundry drop-off, like tablecloths and napkins from late-night catering events, or the dry cleaning needs of servers at those events. Apparently it also, inadvertently, posed a major security flaw.

Something made a snapping sound as a barrel bolt dropped, and then the double door swung open. The figure carefully stepped back with the opening door, withdrawing his arm before he disappeared into the dark laundry.

Melanie stood still in the shadows, even after he disappeared inside, wondering if she should go back into the HR office and call security. But that was a problem.

It might possibly be an employee, going about ordinary hotel business… but if so, why bypass the locks? Why the furtive look before opening the doors, and why did he leave the lights off? The right thing to do was to call security, and to flood the area with lights and attention.

Was she hearing the faint sound of a paper shredder?

On the other hand, if she were to call it in, the incident would get into the security log, and she wouldn't want Kurt and Oleg asking questions about why she was there in the first place. Her duty as a manager of the hotel was in conflict with her mission to find out what secrets the management company had up its sleeves.

The dilemma abruptly ended. The figure emerged a moment later, and she could see that he was reaching back through the opening, setting the barrel bolt that had held one of the doors. The other door closed against it with a spring latch, leaving the laundry exactly as secure as it had been before.

He wasn't carrying anything, and he didn't seem the least bit furtive. If anything had been stolen, it was small enough to be carried in a pocket. As he walked away, he seemed oddly confident, as though being found in the yard, by itself, would not be the least bit suspicious. It was highly likely that he was on the Maintenance staff, she supposed.

He went around the corner of the laundry and got into a parked car, then drove casually away, down the hill. She didn't get a good look at the car, because of the dusky dark. Even with her elevation, the car was mostly hidden by the corner of the laundry.

She frowned. This would definitely need further investigation. Something was rotten in the state of Denmark. Someone was able to access the maintenance and the housekeeping offices at will, despite not having the key – and that suggested that the individual did not have the authorization, either.

But right now, as her immediate priority, she had files to copy and replace in HR, and then, when the current DAT was done uploading to her laptop, she would have more files – electronic files – to copy down in her office. Whatever the odd errand of the figure in the dark, sorting it out could wait.

She slipped down the stairs, and used a proper key to let herself into the laundry, turned on the lights, and then went into the housekeeping office.

Chapter Seven

O WOKE UP IN a cold sweat. The dream had been worse this time. The three men from the bank had followed him here, to this loft. They had stood over him, taking turns shooting him, before one of them handed him a bottle of Xino Chymo and threw him over the rail, onto the cars below.

Except that in the dream, it wasn't cars over the rail, but a cliff that seemed impossibly high. He fell forever, it seemed, and just before the rocks and the waves rose up to crush him, the dream abruptly ended.

He closed his eyes and recited the real facts to himself. The men he shot were dead and buried. They would never show up in his loft. They were powerless to harm him.

It was Jackson who went off the roof with a bottle of Xino Chymo. Whoever it was that threw Jackson off the roof, they were no related to the bank robbers. O was in no danger at all. He was not likely to go over this rail, or off of any roofs.

Not unless he suddenly stumbled onto whatever it was that had gotten Jackson killed. In that case, he might very well do a swan dive holding a bottle of wine, just like Jackson. And with that thought, all of his self-programming was undone.

O got up and put on water for coffee. It was going to be a very long night, and sleep was simply not going to happen.

Melanie had intended to get a good night's sleep, in spite of what she told Kurt. By the time she had copied the personnel files and returned them to Marigold's drawer, the first tape had ended. She sat up all night through the tedious process of loading the tapes, sipping her coffee and reading a magazine as the tape drive did its thing.

By eleven, when the front desk staff were handing off to the night auditors, Melanie was making her way down to the computer room, to put the tapes back. No one would be the wiser, not unless the compared the amount of dust on the various boxes of tapes.

Melanie's laptop went with her to the small suite on the edge of the cliff, where she had taken up residence. She took a quick peek, just to make sure that the files were intact. After all, tapes as old as those might have cracked, or might have been partially demagnetized, maybe even stretched a little. Any of those flaws could introduce errors into files, and render them unreadable.

The files were all there, and the names seemed right, but the acid test would be to open one and find out if the data were readable. And that's where her plan went off the rails.

The files were definitely readable. It was the contents of the file that piqued her interest. She opened one memo after another, stored emails after spreadsheets, and by the time she couldn't bear to open another file, it was already past three AM.

She had expected a few minor irregularities, or possibly something to hold over Kurt's head in order to make sure that the transition went as planned. But not this: these files went far beyond anything she had ever dreamed of finding.

Kurt, and Oleg, and Leon – the latter was her predecessor, it seemed – Oh, but those three had been naughty boys indeed. And she had the evidence, right here. She was tired, and had been up far too late, but as she lay in bed, she still had trouble dozing off. The possibilities for what she could do with these files – they were just so unbelievable.

She could simply upload the files to the secure portion of the Gyannt FTP server, and it would all be over. It would take the better part of a day, with the upload speeds available out here in the boondocks, and it would have the entire office complaining about slow internet connections as a result. But it was possible.

If she did that, corporate would blow the whistle. The sheriff would come, put the executives into handcuffs, and leave her as acting GM until Gyannt sent a full staff to replace her. The transition would jump ahead six months. Gyannt would sue Littoral properties for fraud, and it would be an open-and-shut case. She'd see a substantial bonus at the end of the year, and her career would be golden from now until retirement.

Or she could play the slow hand. She could check-raise, as one of her ex-husbands had phrased it. Act nonchalant at first, and then keep increasing the stakes until someone called. She could set up Kurt and Oleg both, making them commit themselves, and then lay down an unbeatable hand. She was holding all the cards, and there was nothing that could stop her.

Bruce Stanley was the first of the kitchen staff to arrive. The kitchen was dark and quiet, except for the faint hum of refrigerator compressors. He flicked on the overhead lights, flooding the room with light. A quick glance confirmed that the night cleaners had done their jobs. Everything was clean and neat. He walked slowly around the room, ticking things off of his mental checklist.

The refrigerators proper were all at acceptable temperatures. He stepped into the big walk-in, to make sure that everything was properly stored, all food wrapped, all prepared dishes labeled and dated, no raw food above cooked foods.

It was all in order. Pleased, he walked out to inspect the dining room. As in the kitchen, all was in order. The tables were clean, the floors vacuumed, and the linens removed; sent, no doubt, to the laundry. The cabinets in the wine room held the fresh linen that would take its place for tonight's service.

The bus station, between the kitchen and the dining room, stopped him cold. The wine refrigerators were standing open, and the wines were gone. Every bottle was missing. Every single bottle.

He looked around the bus station. It was large, as bussing stations go. There were two double doors into the kitchen, and two into the dining room. The far end was devoted to cutlery, linen, and condiments. The center section, between the four doors, featured serving trays of various sizes and styles. And the near end featured two large glass-front refrigerators, normally stocked with the most commonly-requested wines.

At the end of the room, a smoked-glass window gave a hint of the offices on the other side of the wall, in the secret hallway. Bruce stared hard, and thought he saw motion.

Bruce let himself through the swinging doors into the wine room, and from there, into the little-known hallway separating the wine room from the kitchen. In the chef's office a small man was typing on a computer.

"Hey, Top," said Bruce.

"Yo," answered the man. He looked up at Bruce, showing a small round face carefully shaved with military precision. His mustache met Army regulations, to the very letter. "You're in awful early, Bruce."

"About normal," said Bruce. "You're late getting off."

"Yeah, two guys called in, and we had to rush on the carpets," said Top. "Just leavin' a note for Orin about one of the tables. Got some bad scratches."

"You see anyone messing with the wine refrigerators after closing?" Bruce pointed through the smoked window.

"Just Javier. He packed all them bottles into milk crates and wheeled 'em over to the elevator."

"Say where he was takin' 'em?"

"He didn't say, I didn't ask. But with the doors open like that, I s'pose he was defrosting." Top shrugged, and turned back to tapping out the note.

"Thanks, Top," said Bruce, as he let himself out of the office and headed for the cellar.

The wine bottles were there, safely locked up in the cellar, still in the plastic milk crates. Javier had even tagged them with their shelf numbers and their exact locations in the reach-ins. The reach-ins were kept carefully organized, to prevent expensive wines from accidentally selling cheaply.

At least it wouldn't be difficult to get them back in the right places. Bruce made a mental note to ask Javier about it that night.

Melanie let herself into her office, carefully balancing her keys, her purse, her laptop, and her coffee. One of the great perquisites of working in hotels – a "perk" of the job, so to speak – was that fresh hot coffee was always available.

She'd take an extended break around mid-morning, she decided. A quick nap would be just the thing to make up for her late night last night. But for now, she needed to be in early, to show the front office staff that she was a dedicated early riser. Many parts of Melanie's management style were based on always appearing to be everywhere, all the time.

They wouldn't need her there to guide them; they knew their jobs. It was more the moral support and the punctuality example that compelled her early attendance. That, and, of course, wanting to catch Kurt and Oleg with their hands in the cookie jar.

She wondered what was going on in the executive offices, and decided to find out. She pressed a certain code on her phone, and was rewarded with the sound of Kurt humming to himself. She muted her end, so he wouldn't know she was listening.

For now, using a little-known feature of the phone system to eavesdrop would have to do. Over the next couple of weeks, she would subvert some of the administrative assistants to knowingly or unknowingly feed information to her about what went on in Kurt's office. She idly wondered if the executive secretary was loyal to Kurt, and if that loyalty could be bought. If the price were right, it could be a good move.

For that matter, Oleg didn't strike her as someone who would inspire loyalty. Maybe someone in the Food and Beverage staff could be bought as well. It would be a very clever thing to have the inside goods on Oleg.

She opened up the laptop and started reading the secret books of the hotel. There was a large amount of money sloshing around, mixing and dividing, coming in as random numbers over there, circling around through various accounts, and then seeping out as random numbers over there.

It was as if there were a secret income stream flowing through the hotel. Well, that was one way that an accountant could choose to interpret the data. Of rooms revenue, a certain percentage should be cash. On the books here, the amount of cash was far over that percentage. The expenses, and especially the cost per occupied room, should be a set percentage of the average daily rate, and it was far higher than it should be. Again, a large amount of that went out as cash.

Instead of a twenty-percent CPOR, which would be high in most hotels, and an eighty-percent flow-through to gross operating capital, these numbers were inverted.

She took out her cell phone and sent a text message to her forensic accountant, Reggie Pinn, back in Nashville. *Drop Everything. Come to Inn at River Columbia. Be the Acting Front Desk Manager for a couple months. Need you now.*

With the chill of winter coming fast to Tennessee, Melanie imagined that Reggie would be on the next plane. He was a real find; a graduate of UNLV that she had discovered at a Gyannt Hotels property down in Oceanside. The shift from California had been a shock to his system, so she was sure he would want to be in on a deal like this.

She turned her eyes back to the books. To read these ledgers, eighty percent, or more, of the revenue from a guest room in this hotel went right back out as hard expenses. That was an insane proportion. No hotel in the world could possibly run like that. The remaining twenty percent would not support debt service and capital expenses. And yet, this hotel apparently did run like that, and that twenty percent more than carried the hotel itself.

On a hunch, she pulled up the forms submitted by the hotel to the management group, and through the management group to the ownership group. A quick comparison highlighted the anomaly.

The bottom line was the same, but all the numbers in between were completely wrong. Average Daily Rate was a fraction of its counterpart in the secret files. Operating expenses, likewise, were a fraction. But the bottom line, the flow-through, read exactly the same, to the penny.

A door slammed, and it took a second to realize that she was hearing it through her muted speaker phone.

"Kurt," came Oleg's voice, without any preamble. "We've got to do something about Melanie."

Well, thought Melanie, *A good start would be to disable Hands-Free-Answer-Intercom on your phone system. But don't feel like you need to do that just for my account.* She smiled to herself and raised the volume of the phone speaker.

"She was here all night going over safety records," said Oleg. "I get the idea that she's just getting started. If she finds the secret drives, she's going to get into deep water pretty quickly. We can't let her keep sniffing around."

Too late, thought Melanie. *But run around locking up barns, see if I care. I already have your mare.*

"She doesn't have the slightest idea what's going on," said Kurt. "We'll play her game for now, make her think she's winning, and walk away with … well, you know."

"Yeah, I know. Look, still, we've got to call Louis. He's got to be brought up to speed on this."

"Louis? I'm not so sure. She's just one person. I'm pretty sure we can handle her."

Not likely, thought Melanie. *And once I get my forensic accountant…*

"Not if she figures out all Leon's old tricks. Our fingerprints are all over that stuff. If she figures out where to shoot, we'll be sitting ducks. We need to get the big guys on this quickly. We might need a specialist."

"Are you thinking that she needs to have an accident?"

"I'm thinking that she might need to have a tutorial on how we run the fungus foraging event, and she might need to make a grave mistake in identifying edibles."

"Tragic. Very tragic."

"Not the first time someone's died on a fungus forage."

"You had to throw that in my face."

Melanie hung up the phone. They were plotting her murder. They were casually chatting, in cold blood, about taking her into the woods and feeding her poisonous mushrooms. She felt vaguely nauseous, just at the thought.

Melanie closed her laptop, put her phone and her keys into her purse, and walked out of her office, leaving her coffee behind.

Chapter Eight

"THEY ALREADY KNOW ME down there," said Millie Millie, the misanthrope. "When I went there with O, that Jackson Johns fellow said I was his cousin. To cover why we were really there, naturally. And I still don't know why we were really there."

"And the results weren't very pretty," said Langer, pensively. "You have a point."

"I could go down there and have a late lunch," said Shelley, looking up from her knitting. "It's a lovely view, and the food is to die for. Oh, I'm so sorry, that's so inappropriate."

"I don't like sending one person alone," said Sheriff Langer. "I'll be down there later, but of course you can't be seen with me."

"What about Triple-A?" asked Shelley. "She's good company, and she's exceptionally observant."

Millie snorted, as if the idea of Triple-A doing anything besides sitting at the dispatch console amused her to no end.

"Not a bad idea. We could call in the part-time dispatcher to cover." Sheriff Langer nodded. "I'm not asking you to snoop around, or to ask any questions. Just keep your ears open, and have late lunch, maybe an inexpensive glass or two of wine, then come back. And make sure you spend enough time there to burn up the alcohol before you drive back."

Sheriff Langer stepped out of the tiny break room and turned towards the dispatch room. "Aiden, you up for a road trip?"

Becka was nervous. Her normal daytime sitter had cancelled, and Rina had offered to cover. She knew she should trust her, after all, she had trusted her with a key to the apartment. Still, if Becka had had any choice about going to work, she'd never have agreed.

She'd have to call at lunchtime and make sure everything was okay. And of course, Rina would think she was a nervous Nellie, but when it came to Rachel, well, maybe she was.

The single mother role was taxing, and not having any family to speak of only made it worse. Her mother was around here somewhere, probably, but she wasn't so sure that she wanted Rachel to know her grandmother that well. Crazy probably wasn't genetic, but it might be contagious.

Not for the first time, she wondered if that's why things didn't work out between her and Ben. At first, he had seemed so perfect. He was nice, he was clever, and he had seemed to appreciate her as a person. Did he change, or did she, or did having Rachel change them both? It would probably take a shrink to unravel that mystery.

Rina seemed safe enough. I mean, keeping a three-year-old out of trouble isn't exactly brain surgery, right?

But if that were true, why did she feel so uneasy?

Officer Piedmont frowned. He'd had a lot of people try to get out of a ticket in a lot of different ways, but this was a new one.

"Are they chasing you right now?" he asked.

"No," said Melanie. "But I had to get away."

"Okay, let's back up a step. Did they attack you? I mean, did they physically touch you?"

"Well, no."

"But they want to kill me. They were talking about taking me into the woods and feeding me poison mushrooms."

"You know what? I'm thinkin' you maybe misheard that. They mighta been talking about something that happened a few years ago. A woman at one of these food festivals; she got some bad chocolates, and everyone thought she ate bad mushrooms."

"They said my name. They said they were going to take me into the woods and make me, Melanie, eat bad mushrooms. They want it to look like an accident."

Piedmont had been leaning on the car door, speaking to the woman through the open window. He pushed himself upright and stood for a moment, scowling at her.

It sounded crazy, and he wanted to just write the ticket for speeding and walk away. Still, if he ignored it and it turned out to be something, then he'd look stupid, and the chief would be on him again. He didn't need that.

"Where did this happen?" He asked. "These guys just walked up to you and started talking about this stuff? Making threats?"

"They didn't know I was listening," she said.

Piedmont smiled. It sounded like he had an out: Washington is a two-party consent state. She wouldn't press charges if it got her into trouble for eavesdropping.

"Well, you shouldn't have been," he said. "First, that's illegal. And maybe they were just joking around, and you only caught part of what they said. So I'm thinking that just letting it go—"

"I heard the whole conversation. I know what I heard, Officer. They made a credible threat on my life. A clear and present threat to kill me." She gave him a fierce look. "Don't play this off as hysteria; that's a slap in the face!"

"Okay, okay," he said, trying to soothe her. "Where did this happen? What were you doing?"

"I was in my office at the hotel—"

"Wait. That big hotel down there on the island? Across that bridge? That's where all this took place?" He was grinning from ear to ear. "That's out of my jurisdiction. Tell you what I'll do, though. I'll guide you to a little coffee shop we got here in Ilwaco, and you can wait for Sheriff Langer to send a deputy down here for your official statement."

"Officer, this is—"

"This is not my problem," he said. "But I'll gladly help you get to the right people." That was an understatement: Throwing this mess into Langer's lap would greatly amuse Piedmont.

He tucked the woman's license and registration into his shirt pocket, to keep her from running off. Then he went back to his car and led her into town.

Triple-A smiled at Shelley. "Thanks for inviting me along," she said, before turning her eyes back to the road.

"You're much better company than Millie Millie," said Shelley. "That woman can really get on my nerves sometimes. And besides, you're a much better driver than she is. If she were driving, I'd never be able to relax and knit like this." Shelley glanced up at Triple-A, over her half-moon glasses. "Must be good to get out of that little cubicle, anyway."

"I don't mind it," said Triple-A. "It's kind of cozy. Feels like a protective shell. It's made me think of getting a tiny home."

"Like a house trailer?"

"You know those building projects that architecture students make? It's like an entire home for one or two people, but it's got a footprint of maybe twenty by thirty, or thirty by forty. Sometimes even smaller."

Shelley paused, needles in midair. "Would you be comfortable in something like that?"

"I don't know. I'd have to try it to find out, and then I'd be committed. If I didn't think things through so much, I could have just dived into it. But conscience – you know, 'with-knowing,' well, it's like Shakespeare said. Conscience doth make cowards of us all."

"I'm not sure that's what he meant."

"No, but it fits, doesn't it? I mean, we don't try new things because we know that it could go badly, but if we didn't know, we'd just do it. Maybe he should have said, knowing doth make cowards of us all. That might have been better."

"Talking with you is always enlightening," said Shelley. "By the way, have you heard anything about Arinae?"

"Nothing's come through dispatch."

"Heard anything from O?"

"It's as if he disappeared," she sighed. "But Sheriff Langer keeps telling me not to worry about him."

"Ah." The needles clicked.

They drove on in silence for a while, Shelley knitting as Triple-A drove. The winding highway threaded through the tall trees, drawing them ever farther south. The tops of the trees swayed gently, like dancers, keeping a time that only they could hear.

"Would you mind cutting in the heater, Dear?" asked Shelley, a few miles down the road. "I'm feeling a bit chilled."

Aiden didn't feel it, but she did it anyway, and she supposed that the warm air swirling around her legs did feel good.

"If I had to guess," said Shelley, "I'd say that we're in for a snow soon." She smiled into her knitting. Aiden wondered if it might be a sweater of some sort. Timely, if it was.

Oleg walked carefully around his office, staring intently and deliberately at each object. Nothing seemed out of place. In fact, there was no sign that anyone besides himself had been in the office for weeks.

He lifted his phone and checked under it. No extra wires, no odd unexplained objects. Nothing that might be a bug.

He doubted that Melanie was technical enough to bug a phone, but he wouldn't put it past Gyannt Properties to throw in their lot with the FBI or the Treasury department. They would certainly have people who knew how to bug a phone.

Maybe he was being paranoid. Still, a childhood in Brighton Beach, and a few visits to "the old country," had conditioned him to be very cautious, and to always have an escape plan. In St. Petersburg, he had heard a few stories from people who thought they were perfectly safe, until they suddenly found themselves under suspicion. And then it was too late.

A pound of prevention is worth a truckload of cement, as his grandfather used to say.

When Oleg had convinced himself that it was safe enough, he picked up the phone and dialed Celia's extension, up in accounting.

"Oleg, what do you want?" she snapped.

"Log in as Marigold and see if the files on the secret drive have been tampered with. Check the date stamps."

"Why? Nobody knows about them, and the more we use Marigold's login, the more likely it is that she'll catch on."

"She's afraid of her computer. She has no idea what we're doing. She thinks her spreadsheets print out automatically."

"Still, someone will eventually realize that it's not her."

"I have to be sure. I think Melanie has been snooping where she doesn't belong. And if she has, it's better to throw Marigold under the bus."

"Well, best of luck to her. We had professionals hide those drives. You would have to know that the drive existed, and know its exact name, to even find the files in the first place."

"Should we have encrypted the data?"

"Are you crazy? One little zero flips to a one in the unlock key, and we're out forty, fifty million. No encryption."

"Alright, but check the drive. Make sure the files haven't been accessed. We need some kind of alert if Melanie gets her nose in the wrong place."

"One little woman from the ownership group, and you lose your brains. Okay, sure. I'll have them set up an alert, if anyone touches the wrong files. Happy?"

Oleg smiled the painful smile, even though no one could see him. "Thank you, Celia," he said. Little formalities like that made the world run smoothly; another lesson from his grandfather.

He hung up the phone and stared out the window, into the bus station. People get caught because they overlook details. What detail was he overlooking? What was it that would turn around and bite him?

For example, was there even the slightest chance that the sheriff's office would find out what was really in that bottle of Xino Chymo that took the plunge with Jackson? Or start checking the inventory against receipts, in or out?

Unlikely. The bottle had mostly shattered, and any fluid still in it would be mixed with seawater. Jackson clearly hadn't talked, because the Feds hadn't descended on the hotel like locusts. He was safe enough for now, but what would happen next?

Oleg drummed his pencil on his desk and tried to see which way the wind was blowing.

"Al," said Bruce, "I see you're in early. Would you mind clocking in and going up to the reservations office? I think that night audit and security left some dishes up there."

"Sure," said O. He glanced at his watch. He had about enough time to take care of those few dishes, and then grab a cup of coffee, before he started filling the tanks on the dragon.

He passed Javier in the bus station. Javier looked a little stressed, and with Jackson gone, it was no wonder.

"Javier!" said Bruce, as Javier pushed through the second set of double doors, into the kitchen proper. "What's going on with the wine fridges?"

"Steve had me clean them out so we could defrost 'em and wipe 'em down. A couple of guests complained that their wine tasted a little off. But Steve made the decision."

"That's not his call."

"Well, it seemed like a good idea. And he's the night manager. What was I supposed to do? I couldn't ask Jackson."

"Next time ask me. If I'm not here, call me."

"Sorry. I'm just kinda nervous. Jackson handled a lot of stuff. I'm doin' my best but it's kinda sudden, right? Big shoes."

"Yeah, I hear you," said Bruce, lowering his tone. "Hey, what do you mean, the wine tasted 'off?' Are we talking corking?"

"No, but, well … I mean, like that one cabernet we sell, the one Jackson got a special deal, and it was really good?"

Bruce nodded.

"Three different tables sent their bottles back. Said it tasted all wrong. I sampled each bottle, and they were right. It was like a totally different wine. Like it was too – you know about like iron and potassium in the soil, right? What it does to wine?"

"The wines were that far off? But not corked?"

"Not corked, that's totally different."

"How did you handle it?"

"I gave each table a better wine, and I waited at the table till they tested it. You know, some of the good Ukrainian Stream stuff, out of California; not too expensive, but really flavorful. So they were happy. Everybody likes those."

Bruce nodded.

"But three different bottles, right?" continued Javier. "And they complained to Steve, so he knew about it; normally they just tell the waiter, but one was all, hey, lemme talk to the manager, and another table overhears it and says me too, me three." Javier shrugged at how situations snowball.

"So Steve said to clean out the fridges."

"Yeah, I told him it didn't smell like corking, but he didn't listen. And he's the night manager. So I stayed late and cleaned 'em, had Arne check the mechanical stuff on top, you know, the coils and stuff, but I didn't get it all put back. The wine, I mean."

Bruce frowned. "Put it back now, all except that cabernet. Bring a bottle of the bad cabernet to Orin's office. Leave the rest of it in the cellar."

"I put 'em in the purchasing walk-in. It's not good to let 'em get warm after they've been chilled."

"Make sure they're marked, so somebody doesn't sell 'em by mistake. We don't want this to get any worse."

The night dispatcher, who was working a day-shift to cover for Triple-A, was simply overwhelmed. There was at least ten times the radio traffic she was used to, and at night, the phone almost never rang. It was a lot more pressure.

She wrote a note on a slip of paper, but the phone rang before she could run in into Sheriff Langer's office. She did manage to wave it at a passing deputy, and catch his attention.

"Sheriff," she said, covering the phone with her hand as she gave the slip to the deputy.

The deputy glanced at the scrawl on the yellow note, and walked it over to Langer's door. The sheriff was away from his desk, so the deputy dropped the note onto his blotter and walked away. It fell onto a similar yellow note, and effectively disappeared.

"I should tell you," said Arne Sigmundsson, "That I'm not much good at this."

"Drinking out of paper cups?" asked Bruce.

"Wine-tasting. Telling good and bad and grown-on-the-left-side-of-the-hill, that kind of thing."

"That's not what I need. I need to know... well, look, I need an opinion. Just tell me how it tastes, what you taste, that sort of thing." He handed Arne a cup with water in it. "Here, start by cleansing your palate."

Arne took the proffered paper cup and swished it around in his mouth. Then he leaned his head back and gargled it, before swallowing the water.

"I guess that works," said Bruce, with a shrug. He handed Arne a paper cup. "Sample A. A slightly dry red."

Arne didn't swirl the cup, or sniff it, or do any of the things a true oenophile might do. He simply sipped some of the wine, held it in his mouth for a second, and then swallowed.

"Not bad," he said. "It has that feel, along the sides of the tongue, dry, but you get used to it. Tastes a little bit like bell pepper. And kinda woody, like oak or something."

Bruce nodded. He took the first cup from Arne and handed him the second cup. "Sample B," he said.

Arne sipped the wine, took a small mouthful, and then spat it back into the cup. "That's awful," he said.

Bruce raised an eyebrow.

"You know what? I've tasted that before. When was it?" He thought for a second. "My sister-in-law's daughter, at her second wedding, they served that."

"Your sister-in-law's daughter would be your niece."

"No, on the other side. My wife's brother's ex-wife's daughter by another marriage."

"That's not blood relations," said Bruce. "If there's an ex-wife in that string, why did you even go to the wedding?"

"My wife liked the ex-sister-in-law better than her brother. They stayed friends. So, anyway, it was a complete travesty of a wedding. The groom was drunk when he got there, and the caterer was serving grilled hot dogs. Not even the good ones, either."

"Hot dogs? At a wedding?"

"Yeah, cut 'em in half and stuck toothpicks in 'em."

"With the frilly cellophane , at least?"

"No, just the normal pointy wooden ones. And it was those horrible hot dogs that have that bright red, what is it, red dye number 5? Something like that.

"Anyway, they had a local craft beer that the groom's brother made – horrible stuff. And it tasted like cucumbers, or like soap, the aftertaste, I mean. So I had a glass of the wine. It was out of a box, and I think it said 'Seers-Rowbucks' on the flap."

"You mean 'Sears, Roebuck, and Co?' Like the department stores? They had boxed wine from a department store?"

"No, this was a knock-off. Misspelled. I don't think the real Sears ever sold wine. Not even back in the catalog days." He shrugged. "That's what this tastes like. That stuff, at that wedding."

"Okay, one more."

"Not if it tastes like that."

"Trust me, Arne."

"Alright, alright." He accepted the third cup from Bruce. "Okay, this one's better. It's kind of, well, I'm getting a real fruit flavor. Like grapes and apples, real mild, but not sweet like a fruit juice. More like … well, it's got an alcohol flavor, too. But much nicer. This I'd gladly drink at a wedding."

"Okay, so even though you say you've got no palate, you pretty much picked the wines the right way. The first was a pretty-good table wine; we sell a couple cases each night. The third was a dessert wine, and we sell a bottle a month. The one in between is supposed to be the same as the first one."

"Then you got gypped."

"Yeah, we got gypped. This…" he shook his head. "I wanted to make sure I wasn't crazy, you know? Maybe I've got a cold, or maybe I'm losing my taste."

"If samples A and B are the same wine, I'm the King of France. I don't know what it's worth, or what you call it, but those are not the same."

"Thanks, Arne."

"Okay, so I gotta ask: Why me? Out of all the people in this hotel, you've got a dozen cooks in there that can tell if fennel was grown in San Benito or on Corsica. Why did you call me in here?"

"Because this is hush-hush. These guys wouldn't understand discretion if it screamed at them. I know I can trust you not to say anything to anybody."

"I am the voice of discretion." Arne reached in his pocket and brought out a roll of breath mints. He offered one to Bruce.

"No," said Bruce. "It's actually part of my job description to do stuff like this."

Arne popped a breath mint into his mouth, and on second thought, followed it with a second one. Bruce checked that no one was outside the door, then Arne stepped out of the office and turned right, pushing through the one-way door to the lobby.

The concierge seemed startled as Arne stepped through. Once the door closed again, it blended perfectly into the lobby wall.

"I always forget that that's there," she said.

Chapter Nine

TRIPLE-A SAT ON the banquette side of the table, which gave her a lovely view of the ocean. Shelley, sitting opposite, had a view of Triple-A, and beyond her, the hotel's gift shop. Neither of them had a view of anything that might offer a clue as to why Sheriff Langer had sprung for lunch, and such an expensive lunch at that.

Triple-A smiled. It was such a pleasant moment. At times like this, she liked to simply pause and enjoy life. There was no pressing need to rush back. The room was comfortable. The view was lovely. It simply felt good to sit there, breathing that air.

The day outside was looking a bit gray, and the clouds grew darker as one looked to seaward. They might possibly get a bit of weather on the return trip.

"Shelley," she asked at last, drawing Shelley's attention from a crème brulée, "What do you think of O?"

"Well, as letters go, it's rather in the middle." She smiled. "But you meant our friend Vowel, didn't you?"

"Can you keep a secret? I've got a bit of a crush on him."

"That's not a secret, Dear. Your eyes are like semaphores."

"Do you think I'm being silly?"

"No more than most of us. He's a nice enough fellow, and a good listener. And he's supposed to be wicked smart. Do they still say that, 'wicked smart?' Or was that just from that one movie?"

"I don't know anyone who says it around here," said Triple-A. "I suppose it might be a Boston thing."

"Well, anyway, he's very smart, or so they say. Aside from that, I don't know much about him."

"Millie doesn't seem to like him much."

"Millie Millie is a misanth—"

"No, she's not. I wish people wouldn't say that. She's just very easily disappointed."

"Kind of you to say so, Dear." Shelley renewed her assault on the crème brulée.

Triple-A turned her eye back to the ocean, wondering once again at the majestic power that sent wave after tireless wave to fight to river's current. It made her feel insignificant by comparison, but in a good way; as if nothing should trouble her so long as the mighty Columbia stood at war with the Pacific itself.

"*All the rivers run into the sea,*" she said, thinking of an ancient proverb. "*And yet the sea is not full.*"

"I suppose not," said Shelley, laying aside the spoon. "That was simply marvelous."

Triple-A glanced towards the kitchen, as a steward stepped through the door to pick up a bus tub full of dishes. Suddenly, Triple-A knew exactly why they were there. Everything just seemed crystal clear.

Melanie had been waiting a long time. She had drunk six cups of coffee, and eaten two slices of apple pie. The Sheriff, or his representative, had yet to appear. She looked around the diner for the thousandth time, noting that the waitress was staring at her from the other end of the room.

It would be amusing if the waitress called the police on her. She might end up in an endless loop.

Melanie looked down at her smart phone. Did she dare to call someone? Would that give away her location?

Kurt and Oleg probably didn't have access to cell phone location data. But they might have associates who did, like the Louis that Kurt had mentioned.

She bit at her lip. One call couldn't hurt. Voicemail picked up on the fourth ring, as it should. The only message was from the night before. Steve Sauer had received a reservation request that insisted on room 419, the only room they had with three perfect squares for its digits. Unfortunately, it was occupied. Was he authorized to move the existing guest?

Melanie found the question oddly disorienting.

Hours earlier, she'd have tried to work out a plan. She might have temporarily renumbered a different room, creating a room 149. Or she might have staged a water shutoff, requiring a room move, only to find that the alleged plumbing problem was minor and transient, once the first guest had settled into the new room.

At that moment, however, the problem seemed so trivial as to be surreal. Just when she was in fear of her life – when she literally expected any passing car to produce handguns from the window, to cut her down in broad daylight – just at that moment, someone was asking if she could accommodate an eccentric with a ridiculous ask.

She found herself laughing at the idea. At first it was a silent chuckle, then an audible guffaw, and by the time she clapped her hand over her mouth, it threatened to break out into a roar. She got up and made her way unsteadily to the restroom.

O spotted Shelley and Aiden the moment he stepped into the café, but he gave no sign. Instead, he simply took the bus tub and disappeared, hoping that they hadn't seen him and wouldn't blow his cover.

Had Langer sent them to check up on him? To recall him? To get a report? Well, he had nothing real to report. All he really knew was that the hotel was running as usual. The news about Jackson had been trumped by news about a new manager, Melanie somebody, who was here to convert the hotel to a new management company.

Maybe he should call Langer anyway: No news was still news.

He took the bus tub back to the scullery. Plates got a pre-rinse from the dangling spray hose, and then went into a rack. Silver got a quick rub with gloved hands, to remove any loose food, and then a quick spray before being sorted into narrow round metal baskets.

The metal baskets, in turn, were carefully positioned, upright, in their own green rack, because there wasn't enough room on the one with the plates. Last of all, each glass was wiped around the rim, to remove any lipstick or residue, before getting a pre-rinse, and before being placed, open end down, on the same rack that bore the metal baskets. Then it was just a matter of inserting them into the dragon's rubber-curtained mouth. The conveyor belt inside the dishwasher would take it from there.

As he slid the second basket into the dragon's maw, he noticed Bruce Stanley leading Orin Kaltwasser into the large mop closet behind the scullery. He was carrying something in a paper bag, and it looked vaguely like a bottle.

O moved to the end of the dragon, where he could get some inkling of what they were talking about, without looking like he was eavesdropping. He picked up a white cloth and began polishing cutlery that had already been cleaned.

"This," he heard Bruce say.

There was a spitting sound. "GAH! What was that?"

"We've apparently been selling it as cabernet."

"That—"

The next few words were cut off as the first of the two racks passed under the final rinse arm. There was a loud hiss as scalding water sanitized the plates, some of it flashing loudly into steam.

"Wouldn't do something like that," he heard Orin say. "I've known Jackson—"

The second rack passed under the final rinse arm, rendering the next few phrases undecipherable.

"Go to Oleg with this? He needs to know," said Bruce.

"I'll handle it," said Orin. "Who else knows about this?"

"Javier, Arne, and Steve. Steve got a call on it, during service last night. They complained to him instead of to Javier or to me. But he thinks the reach-in was the problem. I'll let him know we handled it, and that will be that."

"Why Arne?"

"Don't tell anyone, but the man's got a hell of a palate. He put me onto where this came from, and I think he was right. But he won't say a word, trust me."

"I'm sure Johns wouldn't do this. So who do you think?"

"I don't know..."

The intermediate wash tank started to beep as a warning of low flow rate. O stepped over to the dragon and raised the side

96

panel, exposing the tank and the conveyer that passed over it. A cloud of steam billowed up out of it, forcing O to lean away.

The tank was full of debris: plastic coffee stirrers, small slips of paper that had once been sugar packets, and a couple of teabags. Someone had run some racks through without a pre-rinse. O suspected it was Mac.

O stepped on the foot-lever, dumping the tank into the floor drain. The detritus stayed in the plastic floor sink basket, while the water cascaded down into the drain pipe. With the unusual load of paper and plastic in the basket, the floor sink overflowed slightly, creating a puddle around the floor sink. It ran in all directions on the terra-cotta tiles, even though the floor sink itself was now draining away. O shook his head.

Of course a floor sink should be at the highest point of the floor, he mused. *Otherwise, it might get water in it.* O marveled at what passed for engineering in this world.

If the one tank needed to be changed, the others probably weren't far behind, so he dumped those as well. He let the fill water run for a minute or two before closing the foot levers on the drains of the three tanks. Then he dumped the tanks again, to remove any other debris.

Satisfied that the tanks were as clean as he could make them mid-run, he let them fill. The soap dispensers clicked away merrily, indicating that they were treating the tanks, each with its own blend of soaps, disinfectants, and rinsing agents.

While the tanks filled, he stepped back over near the mop closet. The water surging through the fill valves interfered slightly, but he was able to pick up most of the words.

"Why Jackson was killed?" Bruce asked.

"Best not .... about that, leave ... authorities."

"To be related. How ... not be?"

"Don't ... for now."

Bruce and Orin emerged from the mop closet, spotting O immediately. O turned to them with a startled expression.

"How long have you been standing there?" asked Bruce.

"What?" asked O, raising his voice higher than necessary, even with the fill valves going. He reached over and closed the valves. "What did you say?" he asked, in the sudden silence.

Bruce and Orin looked at each other. Orin shrugged, and they walked away.

Well, thought O, *maybe I have something to report after all.*

"This message is hours old," said Langer, to the deputy who stood in front of him. "Couldn't someone, in this entire office, have found me and passed it on? I have a radio and a cell phone."

The deputy shrugged, but he realized that Langer was only speaking to him because he was in front of him. It was obviously a rhetorical question.

"I know, I know," continued Langer. "Not your circus, not your monkeys." He picked up the phone and called the dispatch cubicle. "Who have we got in the south county, close to Ilwaco?"

Shelley and Triple-A were in the car, slightly north of Nemah, when Triple-A's cell phone rang. She ignored it. After four rings, Shelley's cell phone began to ring.

"Well, someone wants to talk to one of us," said Shelley, lowering her knitting to her lap, and reaching into the floor bed for her purse. By the time she produced her cell phone, it too had stopped ringing. The recent calls showed the station house as the last call. She pressed the green button, and listened as it rang.

"Hi, Dear. Shelley with the cold case think tank. Someone there just called – Yes, I'll hold." She pressed the speaker button and allowed the on-hold music, a tuneless strumming of guitars blended with a tuneless tinkling piano, to fill the car. That, and the gentle hiss of the tires on the wet pavement, were the only sounds.

After a moment holding the phone, she opened the car's ashtray and rested the phone in it so that she could go back to her knitting. The ladies listened to the music for several minutes before Langer's voice came on.

"Shelley, are you there?"

"Right here, Sheriff. You're on the speakerphone with Aiden as well." Shelley smiled at Aiden.

"How far back are you?"

"We're midway between Nemah and South Bend," replied Shelley. "About fifteen minutes from the station."

Triple-A thought that that was a generous estimate, and that twenty-five might be closer to the truth, but she let it slide.

"Never mind," said Langer, with a sigh. "It's probably best if I go myself."

O retrieved his cell phone from the tiny locker in the break room, and made his way out the back of the kitchen, down a sun-bleached flight of wooden stairs, and into the small herb garden behind the main building. This still didn't seem private enough – he could imagine being overheard from the pool deck, the employee cafeteria patio, or the small outbuilding that hid the main building's electrical panels.

He made his way past the pool, past the Stone house, and down to a small clearing at the edge of the river. There was a bit of background noise from the river, but that seemed a small price to pay for privacy.

The sheriff answered on the third ring. "Be quick," he said. "I'm out the door."

"O checking in," said O. "A couple quick things. Looks like the sous-chef and the chef are aware of the bottle-swapping. You might want to run background on Orin Kaltwasser and Bruce Stanley. Some diners reported that their wines were off, and Bruce seems to have figured out that the wine wasn't the right stuff. From the sound of it, they know nothing about it beyond that."

There was silence for a second.

"Listen, O," said Langer. "Can you get away for a little while? How close are you to a place called the Ilwaco Nite-Owl Café?"

O walked into the coffee shop, but a quick scan of the nearly-empty room did not reveal Melanie Nador. He stood for a moment, re-scanning the booths and tables.

"Looking for someone?" asked the waitress, from behind the register. "Or do you need a menu?"

"There would have been a lady in here earlier, younger middle-aged, dark hair, business outfit."

"Right," said the waitress. "She sat in that corner over there and she kept looking out the window. She left a couple hours ago." The waitress got out a menu, and held it towards him. "We got a special on the apple pie, if it strikes your fancy."

"No," said O. "I was supposed to pick her up and give her a ride. I was a little late getting the message."

The waitress gave him a sympathetic look. "Hon, you might be a little bit late in getting a couple of messages. She took up with a fellow that stopped through here, and they've been gone about an hour already." She shook her head. "So sorry to be the bearer of bad news."

The waitress didn't look sorry; in fact, judging by her facial expression, the little drama that she imagined unfolding in front of her, was probably her bread and butter. O expected to be the main subject of Ilwaco gossip for weeks to come.

"You wouldn't remember what he looked like?"

"I can't describe him," she said. "I'm terrible at that. But he's in here nearly every evening, about the same time. Gets coffee to go, no cream, no sugar." She shook her head. "I am real sorry this happened to you, Hon, but sometimes, it's best to just let 'em go."

She held out a menu, as if a good plate of corned-beef hash would set the world right.

O nodded, ignoring the menu. "You're probably right," he said. He had no idea what she meant, but he found that the phrase, "You're probably right" was very often a good way to end cryptic conversations. He headed out the door and drove back to the hotel.

Arne looked at the lock. "Yeah, I could probably pick this," he said. "But it would take me a while. I'm pretty rusty."

"Well, get started," said Oleg. "Nobody's seen Melanie since this morning. For all we know, she's lying in there, unconscious, and she needs help. It could be life or death."

"Easiest way to find that out is to look in the window," said Arne. He stood up and walked out of the reservations office, past the front desk, and out the front door. As soon as he was outside, he stepped into the planter bed, careful to only walk on the redwood bark that formed its litter layer.

"Just open the door," said Oleg, following him. "Go back in there and open the door. That's an order."

"I'd have to go up to the shop and get my tools," said Arne, not breaking his stride. "Besides, it's against policies. I'd be in violation. I could get fired."

"I'm the assistant general manager," snapped Oleg. "I'm giving you the order. You're not getting fired."

100

"Well, not just me, then," said Arne. "Both of us. You have read the policies and procedures manual, right?" He stopped outside a casement window with a steel frame, divided into two major sections. Each of the two halves were divided into two columns of four panes each.

Arne peered through the panes. "No Melanie," he said. "So no emergency."

"I want that door open, and I want it open now."

"Can't do that," said Arne. "Policies and procedures." He made his way out of the planter bed and started walking up the hill towards the maintenance shop.

Langer cursed his misfortune. Then he soundly cursed Officer Piedmont, for not calling it in directly. Ilwaco dispatch would have raised Langer in seconds, and he'd have met this Melanie woman while she was still in the diner. She'd be telling all she knew, and maybe even confessing to killing Jackson Johns. He might have been able to wrap up this entire business before dinner.

As it was, he'd have to stake out the diner tomorrow evening, to see this fellow when he came through for his regular coffee.

If he came through. If he wasn't a figment of the waitress' imagination. So who was this Melanie, and how did she fit into things, anyway?

He knew some of the hotel management, from the previous case. He knew Kurt Foulard, the general manager; he knew Orin Kaltwasser, the chef; and he knew Steve Sauer, the night manager. Apparently Oleg Rustoff had come in to replace Leon Rothenberg, who quit and moved across the country. He had never heard of this Melanie Nador, or not until the report came in.

If she was the rooms division manager, then she had taken Oleg's place, and Oleg was in charge of something else.

So, how was this Melanie involved in this whole deal? Was she in on the bottles scam? Not likely, he supposed. She'd have to be involved with food to be able to make it work. So why did she so desperately want to talk to him?

Piedmont's report, as he had managed to extract it from the Ilwaco PD, was vague at best. Langer didn't want to call it laconic, because that would imply a deliberate choice to be concise. The fact was, Piedmont was lazy. He couldn't be bothered to give a detailed report. *Traffic stop, speeding, woman wanted help, manager from hotel, scared of people at hotel. Sent her to diner to wait.*

Langer took a deep breath, shaking his head at the grossly unacceptable excuse for a narrative report.

"Al," shouted Bruce, as O walked into the kitchen. "Where you been? We're stacking up over here!"

There was a pile of dirty dishes on the pre-rinse counter, and as O watched, a waiter came in with another bus tub.

"Smoke break," he said. "But I'm back." He nodded to the dishes. "I'm on it."

O had never smoked in his life. As he once explained it to his doctor, he had never felt the urge to stick burning leaves into his mouth. But the term "smoke break" made a good excuse for frequent or prolonged absences. No one would question it, and some of them might even be sympathetic.

"Let me know when you catch up," said Bruce. "I need you for a special job." Bruce returned to his previous task, helping the salad chef catch up on a surge of demand for Caesars. Once the salad chef was set right, Bruce washed his hands and headed for the bus station, to check things there.

O started sorting the remains of meals into their respective categories, rinsing items as he went. It really wasn't tough work, and it didn't take much concentration. His hands seemed to work independently of his mind, quickly sending the first rack (all plates) and the second rack (all glasses) into the dragon.

Behind them went a third rack (mixed, cutlery and glassware), followed by another rack of just plates. The pile in front of him quickly dwindled. He flipped over a couple of bus tubs and sent them through without racks; the bussers would need them pretty soon, and there were a limited number of them. For plates and glasses, on the other hand, they could turn the entire restaurant at least twice more before even having to dip into the ones reserved for meeting rooms and off-sight catering.

Once the last rack had gone in, and the first racks pulled and stacked to dry, O rinsed down the stainless countertop. Moments later, the swinging door from the tasting room swung open, and Bruce came through, having just checked the cabernet supply in the glass-front refrigerators.

"That was fast," he remarked.

O shrugged. "Guess so," he said, as if not convinced.

"Listen," said Bruce. "Room service is short some people tonight, so we need you to take a cart and swing through the cabins. Hit all the room service boxes, and check for trays outside doors. We don't need to feed the raccoons."

O took the request in stride, nodding to the larger man. "Soon as I stack these last racks, okay?"

The electric cart, a modified gold cart with a large plywood box where the golf clubs would normally be, was almost two wide for the pebbled concrete path. The faint yellow headlight at the front was weak, at best, and did little to help him navigate.

He came around the island clockwise, putting him among the most rustic cabins first. Rustic, in this case, was a polite way to say crude and primitive. Each cabin had electricity and running water, but they were small cabins that barely held the furniture crammed into them.

A raccoon skittered across the walkway, running from O's headlight. Then the attraction that had drawn it appeared: A room service tray lying on the ground outside one of the cozy queen cabins. The cozy queens were a tight fit for the queen beds within; hence the name. There was space enough to reach the *en-suite* bathroom, and not room for much else. Certainly nowhere for a room service tray once one had finished it.

He stopped and picked up the tray off the ground, retrieving the napkin from the flowering impatiens by the door, where the raccoon had dragged it. A ramekin of butter, now licked clean, had rolled into another flowerbed.

Once reassembled, the entire tray went into the plywood box on the back of the cart. O looked around for more debris, but the tiny pagoda lights beside the trail didn't fully illuminate the area. He resigned himself to weaving the unwieldy cart among the cabins, in search of other trays.

A couple of the room service boxes had trays in them, and he transferred these to the cart as well. The boxes were like the box on his cart, and had been designed to give housekeepers a quick way to place trays out of reach of woodlands creatures.

After what seemed like an eternity in the woods, he came to the Stone house. It was named for a writer, Trajan Stone, who had lived on the island long before the hotel had been built. In this rustic structure, he had composed several great novels that forever changed American literature.

The house, from the looks of it, might have escaped from *On Walden Pond*, at least from the outside. The lower half of the outer wall seemed to be river rocks, crudely mortared with a mud and cement cob of some kind, or maybe stucco. The upper half seemed smoother, like a mud mixture, possibly adobe or some other kind of clay. It might have been clay and wattle; the setting was certainly right for a combination like that.

A rustic iron porch lamp hung near a door on each side of the house, as if it had four fronts and no back. There once had been a chimney on the near side, attested to by the mortared stones still stacked to the eaves.

As he approached the Stone house, he thought he saw a movement in the curtains of room 504, the near side of the house. Then the lights went out. The sudden darkness, just as he approached, raised the hairs on the back of O's head. There was something not right about it.

Still, it wasn't his problem. He drove by, the box rattling as he took the cart up the steep winding ramp behind the pool, to reach the loading dock by the kitchen.

Or maybe it was his problem. That was the room where a murder took place, two years ago. The lights went out after someone looked through the window and saw him coming. Someone was hiding something. Something secret was happening.

O dismissed his thoughts as being silly. Many secret things happen in hotels. Most of them are harmless. But on the heels of that thought came another:

And some of them are deadly.

Chapter Ten

"PERHAPS WE SHOULD STEP into the back," said the tall man with the bright red hair. "I rather hate discussing my business in front of the entire world."

Steve frowned slightly, but the man had a point, even though the entire world, at that moment, consisted of himself, Becka, and the man with the slightly odd mustache.

The mustache grew like two small bulbs, one on each side of his philtrum, and the ends were each drawn into a single strand, which curled up on either side of his nostrils. Steve found himself thinking of small onions. Beneath the mustache, the man's chin sported a broad vandyke beard, hiding his pointed jaw in a short, narrow, red cone.

On some men, such a look would have seemed ridiculous, but George Petrovich Herringford III somehow pulled it off and managed to look distinguished and sophisticated. Mr. Herringford was well-known in the hotel; a perennial visitor. He spent large amounts of money, and he tipped well.

Steve decided that letting him into the reservations office wouldn't be a bad idea, even though it was contrary to the normal hotel policy.

"If you'll follow me, Sir," said Steve, leading Herringford through the cipher-locked door. Herringford's quick eyes caught the code: 1-5-4. *The factory default?* he thought. *They couldn't be bothered to change it to something more random?* Herringford smiled to himself at the hotel's naïveté.

Steve led him to a small office beside Melanie's small office. It was intended to be an office for the front office manager and the reservations manager. Since those roles were currently invested in a single person, who was presently on an indefinite leave of absence, it seemed like a good place for a private discussion.

Steve opened the door and ushered Mr. Herringford inside. The tall man took a seat on an office chair with no sides and with a back that wobbled precariously. Steve rested his bottom on the counter and looked at the dapper man.

"I'm sorry," said Herringford, "Did you say that your name was Steve?"

"Yes, Steve Sauer, night manager." *And often daytime front office manager, and sometimes reservations manager, and generally undercompensated for any one of those roles*, he thought, but did not say.

"Well, Steve, call me Red, please. Everyone does." The man's face grew serious. "I'm very concerned about Gyannt hotels."

Steve glanced at the phone, making sure that the red light for the hands-free-answer-intercom button was not lit. He wouldn't want to be overheard talking to an outsider about the conversion.

"Well, we're all a bit concerned with the transition," he said. "This sort of thing is never easy. But the property won't change, and Gyannt has agreed to maintain the tradition of high standards to which we aspire."

This speech was a direct quotation from a memo that had gone around months before, and Steve had said these exact words to at least six other repeat guests. He felt fairly confident giving this statement, since it was literally the official word.

"Frankly, Steve," said Red, with a smile that showed two banks of large, bright teeth, "I don't care about the hotel's standards, and I barely care about its reputation. What I care about is its clientele.

"I don't come to the Great Chefs festival each year for the food or the wine. Those are nice side benefits. I come to visit the sheep, and to see how many I can fleece. I'm a professional gambler; you've surely worked that out."

"Well, your poker games are the stuff of legend," said Steve.

"You've never joined in, have you?"

"I haven't."

"Wise man, very wise, Steve." He smiled again, this time not a toothy formal smile, but a grin of recognition. Steve was one of his kind, it implied, a man with a realistic understanding. Steve was not one of the mugs and punters. These two; they understood each other, as two men of the world might. All this, the grin conveyed. Steve felt as if he were being drawn into a secret club.

"You see," Red continued, in a confidential undertone, "I can generally make as much as twelve or fifteen thousand at one of your food festivals, above my expenses for rooms and meals and such. Your guests are very well-padded, and easy prey. And since I'm only here once or twice a year, you can probably guess that this isn't the only pasture where I use my shears.

"But here's my problem: A change of ownership can mean a change of attitude towards folks like me. We can find ourselves, how shall I say, discouraged from visiting in the future. Even warned off entirely, if the publican is feeling puritanical.

"And on the other hand, the management sometimes just wants a bite of the action. Depending on how greedy they are, that can be a big bite. So it's best to fly under the radar, and if we can't, it's best to know that we have friends in the back office."

"I really can't say what Gyannt would think about all this," replied Steve. "None of us in the hotel really know which way the management will go."

"Well, are the Great Chefs festivals going to keep on? I should be greatly disappointed to lose so fortunate a venue, so entirely suited to my trade. Do tell me that Gyannt will keep them going."

"They've said that they are," said Steve. "Of course, Gyannt is less motivated by the prestige of the hotel, and more by the bottom line. So I guess it all depends on the money."

"Isn't that so for all of us? So, what are your plans, Steve? Are you in this for the long term? Planning to stick around here, maybe move up a notch? Take the rooms division manager job, next time it comes open?"

More like run away and join the circus, thought Steve. *Or get a stake into Silicon Valley, even if it kills me.* "It's hard to say," said Steve. "It's typical for the old management company to move its people to other hotels when this kind of thing happens. But there are often a few managers who stay behind."

"Well, I can certainly understand that, Steve," said Red, his smile now broad and friendly, as if he were hearing what he wanted to hear. Steve almost felt that he had made some sort of promise, without ever intending to.

"Well," he said.

"One should keep one's options open. You're a man who knows when to seize the moment. I see that." Red stood up, and in the tiny office, the only natural reaction was to step back and to open the door into reservations.

"I'm glad we were able to have this heart-to-heart, Steve," continued Red. "I hope that it will be the first of many fruitful conversations." He extended his hand to shake Steve's, as Steve stepped back through the narrow doorway.

Steve found himself holding a handful of paper as Red withdrew his hand. "This way out, then?" asked Red, weaving through the maze of reservations desks and out through the cipher-locked door.

Steve looked at his hand. It held several bills of currency, folded neatly together. He unfolded them and found that he was holding five hundred dollars.

Not sure if that was a tip or a bribe, he thought.

He stepped through the door, into the lobby, and allowed it to close behind him. Red was gone. Becka turned to him and smiled.

"Steve, there was a call from the bar. A guest wanted to speak to you on the deck of the Seaside Room."

Hopefully, not another gambler worried about having a flock to fleece, he thought, as he made his way down to the meeting room level.

"Al, can you stay a little late?" asked Bruce. "We had a small meeting in the seaside room this evening, and they didn't schedule cleanup. Of course, there's another meeting there in the morning."

O shrugged, rinsing the counter after the last of the room service dishes. "Sure."

"Should mostly be coffee cups and a few saucers," said Bruce.

Rina came through from the dining room. "Hey, Al," she said. "Still here?"

"Busy night. Lots to do."

"Yeah, and you probably get decent overtime, too," she said, with a hint of jealousy. She pulled out her cell phone and jabbed at it as she walked through the kitchen to the employee locker rooms.

He grabbed a couple of bus tubs and started towards the stairs. There was no easy way to get a cart up from the meeting room level. The hotel had been designed to follow the contours of the island, and that meant a lot of steps up and down on the lower levels. Which meant that carts were nearly useless.

The seaside room was dark, and O ran into a table. He dropped the bus tubs onto it and began feeling for the light switches. In a room this size, they could be on any side of any of the doors.

There was motion on the deck outside. The seaside room had nothing but tall glass panels on two sides, to take advantage of the marvelous view, as the river swept past, flowing away, down towards the sea.

Someone was walking on the short side of the deck, coming from the herb garden, and moving towards the seaward side. Probably a tourist, out for a moonlit walk, or possibly a cook taking a smoke break.

O found a bank of light switches, flipping three at random just as he heard a muffled bang. It was like the sound of a firecracker. In the light that shone through the glass, he saw a figure, out on the long side of the room, all in black, holding a gun. The figure pivoted towards O, pointing the gun through the glass.

O killed the lights and dove for the floor, as the window out to the deck shattered. Two more firecracker sounds, and two resulting thuds in the wood panels where he had stood.

Was that the shadow he had seen walking onto the deck? No, it was too far away. Two people, one with a gun. An ambush. He scanned the windows. It was hard to see from his low vantage point, prone under a table, but it looked like someone was crouching at the corner of the room, on the side away from the gunman.

The gunman stepped into the room through the shattered window, firing several more times, seemingly at random. He was probably trying to flush O out of hiding, but O's limbic brain told him to lie still and to be quiet. O did exactly that, shielded from even the faint moonlight by the darkness under the table. But if the killer found the light switch, it would all be over in seconds.

There was a crunch of footsteps on broken glass. The killer was moving towards the light switches. He fired another random shot, and in the darkness after the flash, O understood its purpose. The killer was trying to get a glimpse of O in the momentary light.

The crouching figure outside took flight, and the motion caught the killer's eye. Three quick shots went to that end of the room, shattering two windows. The fleeing shadow, whether hit or not, disappeared to the safety of the herb garden.

Voices. There were voices outside the meeting room; excited voices, concerned voices, shouts. The breaking glass and the shots, though muffled, had raised attention.

The killer stood still for a moment, then ran back out to the balcony, and vanished around the end of the room, opposite the way the first shadow had gone.

O lay still, even after the lights came on; even after the voices materialized as people, hotel staff. He listened as they took in the room, the broken windows, and holes in wooden wall panels, in tables, in the artwork on the walls.

He heard a voice say, "There's Al!" and then he started to violently shake.

Steve Sauer made it back inside the main building, darting up the stairs to the kitchen level. Through the kitchen, into the tasting room, into the dark hallway by Orin's office. He took the fire extinguisher off the wall, waiting for someone to come through after him. After several quiet minutes, he hung the extinguisher back on its hook.

He cracked the secret door into the lobby, peering carefully for someone lying in wait. After a couple more quiet moments, he pushed through, letting the door close behind him as he darted across the lobby and into the safety of the reservations office.

Becka watched the sprint with curiosity and concern. She slid the first pocket door open, letting her into the tiny telephone operator's cubicle. Then she slid the second, sticking her head through. Steve was seated at a reservations station, his leg up on the desk. He had tugged his pants leg above his calf, exposing an angry red line across the muscle.

"What happened?" she asked, coming towards him.

"Call the Ilwaco police," he said. "Someone shot at me. Get Piedmont out here."

She turned on her heels and went back to the operator's station. While she was calling for help, Steve tried to bandage his own leg. The alcohol from the first aid kit stung, and he poured too much. Until it dried, the tape wouldn't hold a gauze pad in place. He found an ace bandage, and wrapped it tightly to hold the gauze pad in place over the wound.

Did Becka set him up? Intentionally, that is? Well, as far as he knew, she had no reason to want him dead. She could have just walked into the back office and shot him there.

"Becka," he called, as he lowered his leg and shook his pants leg down over the bandage. She didn't answer, so he limped up to the operator station. He hadn't felt the need to limp, before, but with the bandage on his calf, it seemed natural.

Becka was standing in the operator station, speaking to the handset. "One second, he's right here." She covered the handset. "Are you hurt? They want to know."

"A scratch," he said. "Barely there at all. But we need the police out here, fast. They might still catch him before he gets over the bridge. Hey, the guy who wanted me on the deck by the seaside room – did you see him at all?"

"Nope. Called from the bar." She shrugged and turned back to the handset.

Steve limped to a reservation station near the operator's booth and plopped down in the chair. He called the bar, but the bar never answered during busy times, and they didn't answer now.

The police would check. They'd find out if someone saw the guy. He took a deep breath and reviewed it in his mind. If the lights hadn't come on in the room just as he rounded the corner, he'd have gotten two in the chest and gone over the rail into the river.

As it was, he barely saw the guy in time to react. Whoever turned on those lights, Steve owed him his life.

O was sitting in a chair in the seaside room, looking like the victim of a mugging, or like someone pulled out of a river.

Bruce had hurried down from the kitchen when he heard about it, and he was shocked by the amount of devastation that had

111

occurred in the meeting room. He looked at the shattered glass, and shook his head at the steady breeze that blew through the room. It seemed surreal to him.

"Al, man," he said, at last, gesturing at the destruction. "I just sent you for the coffee cups."

It might have been funny, under any other circumstances, but Al couldn't laugh. They had thrown several tablecloths around his shoulders in place of blankets, but he still felt cold.

"Listen," said Bruce. "Police'll be here any minute. They'll find the guy. They'll take care of him. You're safe now."

Chapter Eleven

"AS SOON AS WE end this interview, you get your stuff and go back up to South Bend," said Langley. "Getting you shot at is over the top. I never meant for you to be in any danger."

"They weren't shooting at me," said O. "They were shooting at someone else on the deck. I flicked on the light at the wrong moment, spoiled the shot, and I guess that the shooter decided to reduce the number of witnesses."

O sat in the general manager's chair, with a folded blanket tossed over his shoulders. He had been cold earlier, from the shock, but now he was warm. He was actually a bit too warm, but no one would let him take off the blanket. It was only partially unfolded, and it lay like a lump across his shoulders.

Langer stood across the desk from him. Another deputy, one whom O hadn't met, sat in a chair by the window, taking notes.

"So let's run through it. You walked into the room," said Langer, with a leading edge.

"I walked in; I almost stumbled over a table in the dark. All the curtains were open. There was a very small amount of moonlight on the deck that goes around the outside of the room. I saw someone walking onto the deck, from the end, by the herb garden... right below where we are now."

"Hair, eyes, height, weight?" asked the deputy.

"Medium height and weight, all in shadow, walking fairly briskly, and seemed to have purpose. Not enough light to really see more about him."

"Him?"

"Had a kind of a masculine energy, if you know what I mean. The movements seemed masculine."

"Then?"

"As the figure reached the corner, I found the switch and flicked the lights on. There was a firecracker noise, fairly quiet for a gun, but still loud."

Langer nodded. "Go on."

"The second figure turned towards me. I hadn't seen him until then. I flicked off the lights and dove under a table."

"Any description?" asked the deputy.

"Tall, thin, mid-tone dark skin through the eyeholes in the ski mask. Quick reflexes." O shrugged, but the blanket hid it.

"What happened to the first guy, the target?" asked Langer.

"He crouched down in the corner, outside, like he was using that stone pillar as a shield, but I could see maybe half of him."

"From under the table."

"Yes. The shooter came in, walked on the glass; I heard it crunch beneath his feet. I have an impression of a black military-style boot with high laces and a high shine."

"How sure about the boots?"

"Fifty-fifty, to be honest. It happened pretty quickly."

"How many bullets?"

"One at the first target, three, maybe four at me as I dove under the table, half a dozen at random inside the room. I think he was using muzzle flash to look for me.

"Then the first target jumped up and ran back this way, towards the herb garden. The shooter fired three or four more times at him, and I think I saw the target stumble."

Through the large window, O could see the crime scene unit examining the short end of the meeting room, and the walkway where the would-be target had escaped.

"Like he'd been hit?" asked Langer. "Limp, shout, stumble?"

"Maybe. But he kept running."

"Then what?"

"People were coming, there was noise in the hallway. The lights came on suddenly; people were pulling me up, to my feet. Exclamations, what happened here, all that. They brought me in here, and Bruce tried to get me to drink a glass of brandy." O pointed to the glass, untouched, on the GM's desk.

Langer picked it up and sniffed it. He wasn't sure why; it just seemed like the right thing to do. It smelled like alcohol.

"Fifteen or so shots in total," said the deputy. "We recovered a lot of .22 long rifle casings. Judging by the sheer number, it would have to be from an automatic."

"We'll know more once ballistics is done," said Langer. "For now, cuff this guy and put him in my car."

Steve Sauer was barricaded into the Front Office Manager's office when Becka brought Langer back to meet him.

"Don't I know you?" asked Langer. He narrowed his eyes at Steve, as though judging where he had seen him.

"We met a couple of years ago. The murders at the Great Chefs festival."

"Right," said Langer. That had been his department's investigation, though he had turned over much of the investigation to a couple of Salinas Police detectives who had been visiting. "You found the body that time. The first body."

"Just now, I almost was the body."

"How so?"

"I walked out onto the deck of the seaside room, and someone started shooting. Grazed my calf."

"What were you doing out there?"

"Becka said a guest wanted to meet me out there, something about a safety concern. So I went down there, started to come around the corner, and all hell broke loose."

"What exactly does that mean?"

"Lights came on in the seaside room, and went back out, I heard shots, and there was breaking glass. I made a run for it, and one shot grazed my calf." He pointed to his leg, where the ace bandage made his calf seem thick under his pants leg.

"We'll have to get that looked at," he said, "We'll need you to come with us."

"I have to stay till midnight and run the hotel."

"We'll have the front desk lady call someone. What's her name? Becka?" Langer frowned, because it seemed to him that she had been mixed up in the previous murders, also.

"We need a statement from her, too," said the deputy.

"I can't leave right now." said Steve. "I just can't."

"You will," said Langer.

Becka gave her statement to the deputy. It was brief: Someone had called from the bar and wanted to see the manager on the Seaside Room deck, urgently. She didn't recognize the voice. It sounded like a man. She didn't hear any accent; there was nothing distinctive about it. She couldn't tell young or old.

She tried to call Melanie, but all of Melanie's phones were going to voicemail. There was no answer on her cell, in her room, or, as a last resort, in her office.

There didn't seem to be any other choice. Reluctantly, she finally decided to call Oleg.

Arne looked at the deputy and narrowed his eyes. "Do you have a search warrant?"

"Don't need it. O gave us permission."

"Who did?"

"Al, the dishwasher. He gave us permission to search his locker. Now cut it open."

"He didn't give you the combination?"

"No, he didn't. I think he was too busy trying to understand his rights. If that's a particular point of curiosity for you, I can read you yours. Now, you want to play lawyer, or you want to cut this lock off?"

Arne hesitated for a moment, but it wouldn't help anything to argue with the deputy. He raised the bolt cutters and snipped the shackle of the padlock. He tried to snip it high up, so that Al could have the maintenance guys weld it back together later on. No reason Al should lose a perfectly good lock over this.

"So Al's under arrest?"

"Happens when you try to shoot people," said the deputy, as he grabbed things from Al's locker and threw them into a box.

"I heard he was under a table when it happened."

"Yeah, but we weren't born yesterday," said the deputy. He looked around, like he was hoping that no one heard anything. "Don't talk about it. We don't need rumors getting started."

"You seriously think Al shot at Steve?"

"See, who told you that the night manager got shot at?"

"It's all over the hotel."

"Well, too bad for Al, that's a really big crime in this state. So is throwing people off of a roof."

"Jackson? You're talking about Al, here? You really think Al killed Jackson?"

"Hey, I told you: don't talk about it. Anyone asks, you don't know anything. I'd hate to have to bust you for obstruction."

"Al?" said Steve, as he got into Langer's back seat. Langer slammed the door and walked around to the trunk.

O said nothing, and tried to ignore Steve.

Steve looked at O, carefully assessing his odd posture. O was sitting his back slightly arched and with both hands behind him, as if he were handcuffed. The look on his face suggested he was barely holding back a string of curses that would make truck drivers blush.

"Al, what the hell?" asked Steve. "Are you, like, under arrest or something?"

"I already told you guys," snapped Al, "I didn't kill that guy, and I'm not saying anything to anybody till my lawyer gets here."

"Al, it's me, Steve."

O was silent, staring through the plexiglass barrier, and through the windshield beyond it.

"Al," repeated Steve, softly. "What the hell is going on, Man?"

O snapped his head to the left, staring Steve in the eye. "Oh, we work together, so I'm just supposed to spill my guts, 'cause I'm just a stupid dishwasher who doesn't know you're wearing a wire?" He turned away from Steve and stared out the window.

The deputy jerked the door open, pulling Steve out.

"Hey," he said. "We can't have you guys in the same back seat. You're a witness. You'll need to ride in my car."

"Why are you taking me in?" asked Steve. "I'm the victim here. The guy was shooting at me."

"Well, you're either in protective custody, or you're a material witness. Either way, we can't leave you here. We'll let the judge sort it out in the morning."

Steve climbed into the back seat of the deputy's SUV. The deputy, once the door was closed, walked back to Langer's car, where Langer was putting O's personal effects into the trunk.

"They buy it?" asked Langer, under his breath.

"The maintenance guy was like a sponge. He's gonna spread it everywhere. The front desk lady didn't seem to like it ... apparently the dishwasher is a nice guy and everyone likes him ... but that's all the more reason for her to tell everybody. I told 'em both to keep it secret. Which means they won't. And the night manager looked like he bought O's act. So we're good."

"Great. By tomorrow morning, the entire hotel will know that we arrested O for killing Johns."

Chapter Twelve

MAYBE IT WAS THE thin mattress in the holding cell, but O's dream was different this time. The three men from the bank robbery were loose, and they were chasing him through the hotel. They seemed to have an unlimited number of bullets to shoot at him, and wherever he went, they appeared.

In the end, he was on the roof. The bank robbers handed him a bottle of Meerwasser Blaues, and threw him off the edge. As he was falling, his leg muscles gave a myoclonic jerk, snapping him awake. He lay there for a while, heart pounding, while he reoriented his mind to the jail cell.

It was too much. His head was pounding with interrupted sleep, and it would do him no good to try to sleep again. The killers would be there, guns in hand. He tried to remember the old dream, the original nightmare, in which he had killed them all. It would have been a relief by comparison. But it was a faint, old memory, and the new dream drowned it out.

The cell did not have the luxury of a coffeemaker, obviously. In fact, he couldn't even sit up all night working crosswords. Sooner or later, he would fall asleep again, and when he did, the dream would return. And it did.

The second time was different from all the rest. There was only one gunman this time. The would-be assassin, who had lured

Steve Sauer into an ambush, instead came through the window, into the meeting room. Except that the meeting room was kind of like the bank, somehow.

The lights would not turn off, and the killer quickly found him. The gun was pointed directly at his forehead. And then he snapped awake for the second time.

"Deputy!" he shouted. When a man in a tan uniform appeared, O said, "I give up. Call Sheriff Langer. I'll tell him what he wants to know."

The deputy disappeared, and O sat down on the edge of the bed to wait. Of course there was no secret to reveal, but Langer knew that. He would move the farce along, pretend that O had been placed on bail, and allow O to go home, where strong coffee and crosswords would keep him from killing people in his dreams.

Bruce Stanley sat in the closed restaurant, watching ships go out to sea. The dark room matched his dark thoughts, and the chamomile tea helped him relax. It wasn't his first choice of teas, and tea was not his first choice in hot beverages, but coffee or anything caffeinated would keep him awake.

Maybe it was time to rethink his life choices. The things going on here were just too unthinkable. Someone tries to kill a steward – a dishwasher – because it turns out that it was the dishwasher who killed Jackson Johns, the best sommelier on the West Coast.

Okay, maybe not the entire West Coast. But the best one Hotel Island had ever seen, that much was certain.

A horn sounded, the deep bellow floating across the water, as a ship coming upstream, bound for Portland, met its counterpart, a motor vessel loaded high with lumber, out of Kelso. Bruce let his thoughts pass out to sea with the latter ship.

Maybe it was time for a change. Ben Corwallis was down in California now, at a place called Old Natividad. There was some kind of diversion program for at-risk youth, training them for jobs in the food service industry. Ben said they needed a new executive chef, and Bruce's resume was certainly strong enough to let him fill the position. It would be a cakewalk next to this.

The moon danced on the river water, making it shimmer.

It might be good to work with Ben again. Ben had been married to Becka, that redhead at the front desk, but apparently that

120

was over. He could barely go to a wedding any more without wondering when it would split up. It was another sad thought, but it wasn't his problem. People make their own decisions, and they live with them.

Ben was cool. He was easygoing, didn't get flustered on a busy night, and he made some great truffles. If he said that the Old Natividad thing was a good gig, it probably was.

Another faint horn, far away, the sound soft and mellow.

It was not a decision to make at one AM, after a rough night in the hotel. That was the one thing Bruce could say for certain. But maybe it was time to give the idea some serious thought.

He drained the teacup and stood up. He'd sleep on it.

Sheriff Langer didn't like the late call, but he only had himself to blame. He should have prepped the deputy before going home. Easy enough to fix.

"Here's what you do," he said to the phone. "You don't finish your logs tonight. Anyone asks why, you blame it on me. Anyone asks about the prisoner, I authorized you to release him at three-thirty AM, on his own recognizance. But you go ahead and let him go now, alright?"

The deputy agreed, and Langer put down the phone.

He wondered if the FBI still had that homicide investigation training course, the one they used to teach out of their Portland office. If he could get a couple of officers to go through that, he might stand a better chance of dealing with that hotel.

If they were going to keep killing people, he'd better prepare.

Becka lay awake, staring at the ceiling. She could hear Rina softly snoring in the other bedroom, but that wasn't what kept her awake. She was trying to make sense of the night's events. Someone shot at Steve, then tried to kill Al, and that led the sheriff to arrest Al and take Steve in for questioning? None of that could be right.

But she saw them take Steve away. Oleg had made her acting front desk supervisor, because neither Steve nor Melanie was available. Melanie wasn't even answering the phone.

And that led to another question: What happened to Melanie? Rooms Division Managers don't just walk off the job. It was weird. There was too much going on, and she didn't like it.

The temporary stipend was nice; it would help with Rachel's preschool. But could she do it? Was she up to running the front office by herself?

She longed for simpler times, which made her think of Ben, back when things were nice. That thought made her think of Ben later, when things were not nice. Soon she was reliving one of their notable arguments, and moments later, she was asleep.

Morning found O walking to Cape Disappointment and onto the bridge, by Dead Man's cove. He might have found the walk relaxing, under other circumstances. The sky looked clear, for now. The air was brisk, and the trees gave a scent of pine and freedom.

This particular morning, O was not dressed for the chill, so he found himself stomping his feet and rubbing his biceps to stay warm. The power-walking helped, but it wasn't enough.

Normally, he'd have dressed warmer than this for a walk in the crisp morning air, but to do that, he'd have to drive back to his loft and get his boots and his jacket. And to do that, he'd need his car. And his car was down on Hotel Island.

He'd gotten a deputy to drop him at the Diner. It looked like it might be open, but he didn't check. If the nosy waitress had seen him, she could add it to the ballad she was composing about him.

The chill got him jogging, and jogging made the long bridge seem shorter. He actually found himself slightly warm by the time he came to a walk in the circle driveway, in front of the hotel.

Micah, one of the valets, trotted up to him. Despite the chill, Micah was wearing short khaki pants and white sneakers. He would burn enough calories running after cars to make up the heat loss.

"Al," said the valet. "You can't be here, man. Not after what happened. They said, if you showed, to call the cops."

"I gotta get my car," he said, turning towards the wastewater plant and the employee parking area beyond it. "Then I'm gone."

The second person to spot him that morning was Marigold, the HR director. "Al," she said, as she emerged from her car, starting to give him the same rebuke as Micah had given. Then she paused, with her rebuke only half-voiced.

Maybe it had dawned on her that he was just picking up the car. Then again, she might have realized the foolishness of speaking sharp and unnecessary words to a man who was accused of shooting the night manager and throwing the sommelier off of the roof of the restaurant.

Either way, she stood still, in the open door of her car, as Al's tiny Vega backed out of its slot and puttered gently up onto the bridge. She was still staring when she disappeared from O's mirror.

Getting the car had served the case, it seemed, in addition to serving him. It would be one more reason for the hotel staff to spread the rumor about his arrest. The alleged killer had had the audacity – can you imagine? – to show up and get his car.

Triple-A walked into Sheriff Langer's office and closed the door behind her.

Langer looked up at her, his eyebrows asking what he could do for her.

"Sheriff, the news was talking about that hotel today."

"Yes, and that has nothing to do with you."

"I know why you sent us down there, me and Shelley."

"And why was that, pray tell?"

"To make contact with O, and to see if he was alright. But clearly, he wasn't. You shouldn't have used him like that. He's not a sworn officer, and you have no right to put him undercover."

"It's none of your business, Aiden."

"It is my business. It's everyone's business. You don't get to act like you're a king, and just hand out the orders."

Langer took a deep breath. "Aiden, how long have we known each other?" He didn't wait for her to answer, but gestured towards a chair as he continued. "I don't always tell you what I'm doing, but I've never let you down, now have I?"

Triple-A declined the chair; She didn't feel like sitting, and it wouldn't have fit her anyway. But it was a nice gesture.

"O knew what he was getting into, and he went in with eyes wide open. And now that it's blown wide open, I'm pulling him out. I've given him orders to move back up to South Bend. He's done."

"Given him orders? He's a civilian."

"He's acting as a posse of one, under my authority."

"So you arrest your deputies."

"Aiden, don't you say a word to anyone about that. It's to draw them in, those hotel people. They're not like us. They don't belong. They're trouble, and they're up to something, and I've almost got them."

"If O gets hurt…"

"He's fine, and what's it to you, anyway?"

"O is my friend. I take it personally when my friends are in danger. So you be careful, Sheriff."

She pivoted on her heels, surprisingly lightly for such a large woman, and flowed through the door.

Langer stared after her for several seconds. He had never seen her with so much fire in her eyes. He had been threatened by many people, most of them far more dangerous than Aiden would ever be. But for some reason, he believed her. It would be a really bad idea to cross her.

Before that thought was cold in Langer's mind, a deputy poked his head in through the door. "Hey, Sheriff," he said, "Sorry to interrupt, but this came through red hot. You know those bullets we got out of the wall of that hotel?"

"One was pretty much intact, right?"

"Yup. We ran rifling patterns through the NCIC database. That pattern came back to a Colt Woodsman .22 pistol, 99-plus percent match. And that's a problem."

"Why is that a problem?"

"According to the California DOJ that pistol was destroyed."

"Like, lost in a fire, dropped into a lake by hunters, that sort of thing? Or …"

"Nope. The chamber and barrel were cut open with an oxy-acetylene torch. Gun was certified destroyed by the welder and a witness. The metal was sold in bulk as scrap to a dealer out of Castroville, California."

"Who destroyed it?"

"Under the order and supervision of the Salinas, California, police department."

Langer shook his head. "Salinas? Seriously? Tell me that…"

"I just got off the phone with a Lieutenant Jones. He's gonna be on the next flight to Portland."

Langer breathed a sigh of relief.

"Well, look who's here," said Shelley, as she walked into the break room. "I almost thought you'd quit the think tank."

"Nope," he said, stirring his coffee.

Millie walked in behind Shelley, and gave O a scathing look. "Finally decided to show up?"

"Yup," he said. "By the way, you can close the case on Arinae Fletcher. She's been seen, alive and well, and acting of her own will. So it looks like her disappearance was completely voluntary."

"How can her mother reach her?" snapped Millie.

"She can't, and that, I think, was the point."

"I can't tell Diane that!"

"Then don't." He shrugged and drank from his coffee. It was the same as it had always been, but he had gotten used to the hotel's better brand of beans.

"So you just saw her walking around South Bend, is that it?" asked Millie. "And you stopped her, identified her, and asked if she was under duress?"

"I told you what I know," said O. "She's alive and well. She's living on her own, acting on her free will. Enough said."

"That's not enough and you know it," said Millie.

Shelley knitted quietly away, grinning from ear to ear. Millie turned to her, took offense at the grin, and narrowed her eyes.

"You think this is funny? Is this some kind of a rebellion? You two think you can run this think tank without me?"

Millie threw her clipboard onto the table and stormed out. O took another drink of his coffee. Shelley knitted one and perled two before turning to O.

"She's down at that hotel, isn't she?" asked Shelley, peering at O over the top of her glasses.

O nodded. "But don't spread it. She clearly doesn't want her mother coming after her."

Shelley turned her attention back to her knitting. "We can't help what's in our DNA," she said. O wasn't sure if the pun was deliberate, so he let it ride.

"Oleg, I expressly told you NOT to call Louis! We're trying to keep this quiet, and now it's blown up in our faces."

Oleg sat calmly in the chair by the window of Kurt's office. "Calm down," he said. "It's not a big deal. I'll talk to Louis, and he'll clean it up. His contractor, his problem."

"Why did he send someone after Steve, anyway?"

"Steve knows. You read the night manager's report. Three bottles reported as 'Off.' He's got to know that the wines are being switched. The roof is starting to cave in, so it's high time for us to find our parachutes."

"No," said Kurt. "It's not time to bail out yet. I'm sure that we can..."

"Javier's a problem, too. And if he talked to Bruce or Orin, then we're in damage control territory. We might need to have a kitchen fire."

"You don't mean..." Kurt envisioned an explosion in the kitchen, a fireball that would wreck the building and end the Inn's usefulness forever.

"You can't bake an omelet without breaking some legs," said Oleg. "We all knew this day might come."

"No," said Kurt. "We're nowhere near that desperate."

"If the lid comes off, and someone finds out about the deal, we'll have ATF on one side and Louis on the other. So a good kitchen fire might solve all of our problems."

"Do you know for sure that this was Louis' doing?"

"I haven't called him since last night, but who else?"

Kurt thought for a moment, and not for the first time, his lack of imagination failed him.

He looked past Oleg, out through the window, where gentle flakes seemed to be filtering down out of the sky. There was something Leon used to say in times like these, about spending the winter in our disco tent. Kurt supposed that Leon was right: The one thing that could make this worse would be bad music.

Chapter Thirteen.

O HAD THE DREAM again. As O came out of the restroom, he saw that Aiden, Rina, and Shelley were in line at the bank, waiting for some sort of a transaction. The killers, One, Two, and Three, were in their usual places. One looked vaguely like Kurt Foulard, but taller. Two could have been Oleg Rustoff, but O didn't see his face.

O grabbed for Two's pistol, but it fell out of his hand, skittering across the floor. Two swung his shotgun behind him, without looking, and shot O one-handed, right in the chest. As O fell, the other two killers opened fire on the customers and the tellers with their AK-47s.

O snapped awake with a snort.

He was in the South Bend Diner, overlooking the waterfront. It was almost eleven. The eggs and bacon in front of him were untouched. His coffee cup, three-quarters full, was in his right hand, which rested on the table. He shivered at the sudden chill that ran through him, despite his jacket.

The waitress came over, coffee pot in hand.

"Let me warm that up for you, Sweetie," she said. "Must have been a long shift, huh?"

O just nodded as she topped up his coffee.

"How about you let me call you a taxi? I'll wrap up your breakfast to go."

"I'm good," said O. He pulled himself upright in the booth and unwrapped the knife and fork from the paper napkin. "I think that nap was what I needed."

She walked away, uncertain, as he cut open the eggs and began to eat. They were still warm, so he hadn't conked out for long. Just enough time for a quick dreamlet.

He couldn't let them do it.

Who? He couldn't let who do what?

He drank deep of the coffee, even though it was really fairly horrible. He needed the fog to lift. He knew that there was something important that he needed to know, something he had to think through, something that he desperately needed to understand. But his brain was broken.

Sleep deprivation, bad dreams, and too much adrenaline were all taking a toll on him. He felt like there were fuses blown in his frontal lobes. He could actually feel an ache in his forehead each time the door of the diner squeaked open.

The coffee at the sheriff's station had done nothing for him. He wondered if Millie had gotten there first and made decaf. Maybe the eggs and bacon would help. Bacon was good for the glial cells in the brain ... made them glide ...

He snapped his head to clear it. No. He couldn't nod off. Not now. There were thoughts that needed to be thought. He wolfed down the eggs and bacon, gulped the coffee, and set the cup at the edge of the table, for a refill.

Outside, small white flakes started to sift from the sky.

The bell at the door jingled, and Aiden let herself in. She spotted O and made a beeline for his booth. "Thank goodness you're alright," she said. "I've been worried."

O smiled. "Thanks. It's good to know that someone's got my back." He motioned for her to sit down. With an economy of motion, she seized a chair from a nearby table and put it at the end of the booth, rather than trying to squeeze into the seat opposite O.

"Have you had any sleep? You look like a wreck."

"My brain feels like the Edmund Fitzgerald."

"Please don't sing that."

"Thank you for asking. I won't." The waitress came, refilled his coffee, and raised an eyebrow to Aiden.

"Coffee, please," she said. "Black is fine."

"Can I tell you something in confidence?" he asked.

"My lips are sealed."

"I have bad dreams. Horrible dreams. I'm back in the bank, and it's being robbed. And depending on how the dream goes from there, either I shoot three people and save the rest, or we all die. Since the thing with Millie, the..." He paused and drank some a gulp of coffee. "When we thought she got bad wine?"

"Down at the hotel."

"Right. Since then I'm having the dream, probably every night or every other night. And with the stuff in the hotel, it's getting worse. Last night, after someone shot at me..." He automatically dropped his voice on the last four words, looking around to be sure no one was listening.

The waitress brought Aiden's coffee, and topped up O again. He added more sugar and a slug of cream before he went on.

"Anyway, last night I couldn't sleep at all. I kept seeing the bank robbers and they kept throwing me off the roof." He put his hand over Aiden's where it rested on the table.

"There's something that I'm supposed to know, and I can't figure it out. It's the key that will open up this case. But my brain isn't working. I'm stuck."

"It's the dream, right?" said Aiden. "It's keeping you from getting to the truth, right?"

"Yes. Without it, I could sleep. And if I could sleep, I'd be able to reset my brain, come at it with a fresh mind. It's just a matter of doing the right math. But I can't sleep, so I can't think."

"I have faith in you, O," she said. "I think that you can change the dream. I think that you can use it." She looked at her watch. "I need to get back to work," she said. "But I have faith in you." She rose gracefully and carried her coffee to the counter, where the waitress poured it into a paper cup for her.

O sat for a moment, staring at the coffee cup in front of him. Aiden had done something miraculous. She had lent him a moment of clarity. She had pierced through the fog, if only for a second.

"Check, please," he said.

"Arne," said Oleg, "I keep getting complaints about work orders from the executive housekeeper. She says she turns them in and they never get done. She's had pink slips that are weeks old."

"Hmmph," said Arne, as if it were news to him. "If you have some pinks I can take the numbers and match them to the work orders. Find out if we're waiting on parts or something."

"She didn't have any to show me. I'll ask for them. But you need to respond to work orders timely. We can't have weeks and weeks of wait time."

"Show me a delayed work order," said Arne. "I'll get right on it. Or just tell me the number."

"Get with her and take care of this," snarled Oleg. "If you can't do your job, we'll find someone who will."

Arne smiled. "I'll get right on it," he said.

"And how long before we can have the heaters fixed in the Stone house? We can't have those rooms off-market for very much longer. We're losing money."

Sure we can, thought Arne. *We're going into the slow season, with an average occupancy of 23%. We won't need those rooms before Christmas.*

"Contractor is waiting for parts," said Arne. "We're currently scheduled for three weeks from now."

"Can you get it done in two?"

"Not without the parts," said Arne.

"Don't give me that. Get those parts here, and get it done in two weeks. Three is just too long to be out of order."

"Sure," said Arne. *All it really takes is a time machine, to make a three-week delivery turn up in two. But sure, why not?*

"If I need to yell at someone to get it done, you just give me the number," said Oleg.

"Will do," said Arne, with no intention of ever doing any such thing. "You'll be the first call."

"Now get those work orders taken care of. Next time she calls me, this won't be such a friendly talk."

Arne let himself out.

He knew why the executive housekeeper didn't have pink slips to back up her story. She had been hoarding them, even after the work was finished, so that she could bad-mouth Arne to Oleg.

Oleg wasn't one for listening; to him an accusation was the same as a conviction. So Arne made it a habit to break into the housekeeping office a couple times each week and to shred all of their pink slips.

It had seemed like a good job when he took it, but honestly, he was wondering if he ever should have left the Chien-Verte Inn, down in California. Among other things, it never snowed there.

O walked into the Sheriff's station. He took a deputy aside.

"Listen," he said, in an undertone. "I need a favor. I can't drive home right now, but I need to sleep."

Ten minutes later, O was locked in a cell, settling his head into the pillow on the bunk. Two or three hours, that's all it would take. Then he would have the answers.

When the brain is a tool, sleep is a weapon.

He dreamed the dream, but it was different this time. He smiled to himself.

"Orin, Javier's not in yet."

Orin glanced at his smart watch, then looked Bruce in the eye. "What time is he normally in?"

"Usually by two."

"It's only half an hour. It's starting to snow out there, and you know what the first snow is like. People forget how to drive."

"We're also down a dishwasher. I'm having Mac work a double, but we can't do that all week."

"Al's out for good?"

Bruce shrugged. "HR wouldn't say. He's suspended pending investigation."

"Don't we have any backups?"

"Couple of part-timers, but I can't get ahold of them tonight, and they have day jobs anyway. We can probably cover this week, but it's gonna be touchy."

"Alright, if anyone wants wine advice tonight, you cover it. Stick to stuff we know is the real McCoy. Maybe one of the room service people would be willing to take some overtime hours on the dishwasher."

Bruce frowned as he watched Orin disappear into his office. Covering for Javier wouldn't be tough, but patching the holes in the schedules wasn't going to be easy. And he'd still have to keep an eye on the cooking line.

Rina watched as the tiny white flakes drifted out of the sky, settling gently on the cars in the employee parking area. She hoped the snow wouldn't make it difficult to get home. If the bridge got iced up, there might not be any way in or out of the island.

Not that she had anywhere to go, but she didn't really like the idea of having to stay in the hotel, and maybe wind up sleeping on a cot in a meeting room, with the other hotel staff. But there was nothing she could do.

She was on her split-shift break. It would be a good two hours, yet, or even more, until anyone was looking for her in the dining room. Not enough time to go home. Plenty of time for a leisurely walk around the island.

The gravel in the employee lot was still dry enough to crunch underfoot. Off to the left, the waste water plant was lit up. Suddenly, as she made her way through the cars, she saw the light go off. Just when she reached the concrete walkway to the remotest cabins, Oleg emerged from the plant, looked around, and then walked briskly towards the main lodge.

None of her business, she supposed. The snow was starting to make a thin transparent icing on the concrete, and when she looked over her shoulder, she could see her footprints, like transparent wet spots. The thought of making a snow angel occurred to her, but the snow wasn't thick enough yet. In fact, it might stop entirely and melt off by tomorrow; that's what the weather app had said.

Up in South Bend, her mother would've been blowing up her phone by now. The idea of Rina out in the snow – as if a little moisture would melt her. Not that her mom would care; once she was safely home, she'd have been ignored, like always.

Rina paused between two of the cabins, with a view of the rocks at the east end of the island. There, the river split. Most of the water went around the island to the south, but a steady stream made its way around the north side.

It was too fast and too cold to think about swimming it, but the channel was too small for the huge ships that made their way along the river. They would almost certainly bottom themselves in the mudflats, or scrape against the pilings around the bridge supports. She turned to the left and stared for a while at the channel, wondering if it might be possible for a ship to squeeze through. No, of course it wouldn't.

With a breath of the brisk air, she tugged her woolen hat tighter over her ears and thrust her hands deep into her jacket pockets. Time to consider getting a pair of gloves. Maybe she'd look around to see if the thrift stores had any. For that matter, they might even have some cute little mittens she could give to Rachel.

She started a slow stroll, clockwise around the island. To her right, on the inside, a granite hillside rose steeply. The rock outcroppings mingled with stands of pine and birch, working in concert to hide the administrative buildings higher up the hill.

Rina had only been up there once, to see HR when she was first hired. It was kind of neat to know that up there, in what appeared to be just more wild space, there were hidden buildings.

To her left, small rustic cabins sometimes blocked her view of the river. Some of them were so tiny, she wondered if it was fair to ask the kind of prices that the hotel got for those little rooms. But according to Becka, people paid it without even blinking.

In time, she came to the Stone house. She had heard of Trajan Stone – who hadn't? But she had never read any of his books. There was just something very unimpressive about a writer from here in this local area. Maybe if she was from Portland, or Seattle, she'd love his work and rave about it, like everyone else did. But Rina wasn't much of a reader, anyway.

There was the octagon, an eight-sided structure with three floors, featuring twelve rooms in total. She had no idea why it was octagonal. Becka said it was some kind of a 60s art thing.

Then she was near the pool, and the poolside rooms; past them, the herb garden, behind the kitchen. Maybe she'd hang out in the break room for a while, or have a cigarette under the deck. Then again, she could go hang out in the reservations office, and see if Becka was busy. By her phone's time, she still had an hour and a half to kill.

Becka was busy. She kept looking for Steve, even though she knew he wasn't going to show up. Reservations had started to come in for the holiday season, and she only had one front desk clerk. The other had called in sick.

Snow flu, most likely: A reluctance to be the first drivers on slick roads. But there was nothing she could do about it. She tried to catch the reservations calls if she could, but the majority of them seemed to be going to the external service. Oleg hated that, because it cost more per call, and they charged the hotel whether they converted the call or not. Becka tried not to let it happen.

The actual desk was just busy enough not to let her do either thing well. People would appear just often enough to keep her from staying in the back. Rudy, the other front desk clerk, was taking his sweet time with each transaction, as if he had no sense of urgency at all, so she kept having to come and help the next guest.

For the millionth time since Oleg had appointed her to the position, Becka felt absolutely inadequate.

"We've got to go back down there," said O, as he swept into Langer's office.

Sheriff Langer looked up at him. "It'll blow your cover."

"I know what the missing piece is. I know where Melanie Nador is. If we can get to her, we'll have it all."

"Have it all?"

"The entire case. All the pieces."

"Which – who killed Johns, you mean?"

"And who's been switching the wines, and who tried to kill Steve Sauer, and who tried to kill me. It's all in the files, and one person has all of those."

"You seem certain."

"Melanie Nador went missing right after she called us to report that she was threatened with murder. We don't have her. We assume that they have her. But they don't."

"Why not?"

"Because someone picked her up from the diner in Ilwaco, and whoever it was, she was glad to see them." O nodded. "The waitress thought that she was running off with another man."

"Another man?"

"Not me, that is. The waitress assumed we were lovers, and that I had showed up a little too late, for the last time."

"I'm missing the connection."

"If Melanie was removed by force, she wouldn't have thought it was a lover's tryst. She only thought that because Melanie went along gladly."

"Ah. So who picked her up?"

"I should've had that too, but I've been so sleep-deprived." He shook his head. "It had to be Steve Sauer."

"Sauer's in on it? He shot at himself?"

"No, of course not. He's been hiding her. He goes to the diner every evening, and gets coffee on his way to the hotel."

"Why not get his coffee at the hotel?"

"Apparently, it lets him procrastinate. But the important thing is this: the waitress knows him on sight."

"And so does Melanie. So when she's waiting, scared witless, and he drives up, she latches onto him."

"With enough relief that the waitress thinks they're lovers. And that's probably the real reason he was nearly shot, not because he knows about the wine."

"Of course," said Langer, standing up and reaching for his uniform jacket. "So we need to get to Sauer and ask him where she's hiding. I'll call the protective detail at his house, so they'll know we're coming."

"No need," said O. "I know where she is."

Chapter Fourteen

UP THE RIVER, NEAR Longview, three ships shared a berth. They took turns; each spent up to 60 days loading lumber before making a run to West Pacific ports, where that fine Washington wood could be transformed into expensive buildings and furniture.

As each ship made its way to sea, her sister would pass alongside her at the river mouth, returning for another load. MV Thousand Rivers was pierside at Longview now, preparing for her westward run. MV Thousand Streams was now passing Puget Sound, moving down the coast. Somewhere close to the port of Vladivostok, or maybe near Inchon, MV Thousand Branches was offloading her cargo.

One more night on the pier, and then Thousand Rivers would cast off all lines, making her rendezvous with Thousand Streams near the old Cape Disappointment light.

The schedule was carved in stone, immutable. As it had been, so it would always be. And Oleg was counting on that fact.

The dry cleaner pushed the rolling basket out of the elevator and across the kitchen, as he had done hundreds of times before. In the tasting room, he made a right turn and took a discreet peek into the darkened hallway before rolling the big cloth basket into Oleg's tiny office. Oleg closed the door behind them.

Then Oleg struck his head with a full bottle of Castelo Não Beber. The dry cleaner went down in a heap. Oleg could hear him breathing, but honestly, he didn't care if the man was alive or dead.

On the computer screen, the transfer of funds was almost complete. This was the end, he knew. There was no turning back. He'd need to disappear and it would need to be forever. The money in the hotel's secret accounts would be enough to let him live like a king in some remote corner of the world, but even so, there was no reason not to take along the present shipment of unwashed cash.

He would need some throwing-around money. There were hands to be insulated with nice warm Franklins. The loading officer and the berthing officer of the Thousand Rivers were going to want to be compensated for putting him into a comfortable stateroom and denying his presence to the customs authorities. There would be luxuries to be purchased, and small comforts to make the long voyage pleasant. And in Vladivostok, when he finally set foot again on *terra firma*, there would be officials to bribe there, as well.

Oleg was a little nervous about that part: The Russian he had learned in Brighton Beach had always seemed a little off during his visits to the old country. Hopefully he was close enough, and no one would start something over his American accent. He would need to blend in, and make himself comfortable without making himself well-known. But that was a bridge to be crossed too far.

He threw off the layer of tablecloths that covered the boxes. There must have been twenty five or thirty cereal boxes, all stuffed full of currency. The weight of each box was marked on the side. For the combination of mixed bills that they normally received, the dollar amount could be calculated with a simple formula, plus or minus a few thousand.

Oleg guessed, from the total weight, that there was probably three and a half million in the basket, give or take. Too bad he couldn't take it all with him. There wouldn't be room in his briefcase. He dumped the first box onto the desk, sorting through the bills and grabbing hundreds and fifties. Those, he shoved into his briefcase in a loose pile.

The briefcase filled way too quickly, and anyway, it seemed a shame to miss all those lovely twenties. There was a wooden crate of wine in Orin's office, so Oleg commandeered it. He dumped the bottles on the floor, except one. He recognized the cobalt blue glass. Meerwasser Blaues. A 1936 vintage, at that; the rare one. He left it in the crate as he stuffed the rest of the space with loose bills. When it was packed as tightly as he could manage, he hammered the lid on with his bare hands.

There was a hand-truck in the bus station, and it only took a few seconds to dash over and grab it. He stood the crate on end, slid the hand truck under it, and put his briefcase on top.

Now it was just a matter of watching electronic money change hands. He turned back to the computer screen.

Reginald Pinn, whose old friends down in South Central had referred to him as Reg, got out of his taxi and looked at the Hotel's main building with great interest.

It was a grand building. It was constructed of rock masonry; not round stones crudely stacked like the Stone house, but random shapes carefully and precisely fitted and mortared. It was a building clearly designed by a master. It was made to fit into its surroundings, and to give the air of an old Scottish palace, or perhaps a Bavarian castle.

The thin white dusting of snow over the building and the gardens just added to its allure. Reg wasn't certain, but it was entirely possible that he had never seen so lovely a building in his entire life.

He smiled as he pulled his suitcases up the winding walkway to the tall wooden front doors. This would do nicely. It would be a simply lovely place to make himself at home.

The suitcases made a rattling noise on the hardwood floor. He parked them facing a wall and stepped up to the redhead at the front desk. She gave him a warm smile and a look of curiosity.

"Excuse me," he said. "I'm Reggie Pinn. I'm looking for Melanie Nador.

"Aren't we all?" muttered a clerk standing behind her, before disappearing through a pocket door into the back.

"I'm terribly sorry," said Becka. "Melanie isn't available just at the moment. Is there anything I can help you with?"

With which I might help you, thought Reg, but he kept from saying it. At UNLV, careful grammar and precise enunciation was the rule. But as he had learned in his many long years down in Oceanside's Sur Playa Plaza hotel, the real operation of a hotel seldom matched the textbooks.

"When do you expect her back?" he asked.

Becka didn't know how to answer that, and he read it in her face. He hoped nothing bad had happened to Melanie, but he knew that he'd never find out from the front desk clerk.

"Is the general manager in?" he asked, and saw immediate relief in her expression. Her face relaxed and her professional smile returned. Whatever had happened to Melanie, at least it wasn't the entire management staff.

"Yes, Sir," she said. "To your right, here, then there will be stairs on your left. At the foot of the stairs, turn right, and it will be the first door on your left."

"May I leave my bags up here?" he asked. Becka smiled and nodded, and she watched intently until he was around the corner before grabbing the phone to alert Demetria, Kurt's secretary, in the executive offices.

Precisely where Becka had described it, Reg found a door marked "Executive Offices." Reg opened it and stepped inside.

"Mr. Pinn?" asked the petit blonde at the desk outside the General Manager's office.

"Yes," replied Reg, impressed that Becka had so quickly spread the word. "I'd like to see the General Manager, if he's available."

"May I ask what this is about?"

No, thought Reg. *It's, 'Do you have an appointment?' and if not, 'Might I ask your business with him?'*

"I'm here to report for duty," he said. "Melanie Nador hired me as her Front Office Manager."

That wasn't strictly true. His job title for the next six months or so would be Front Office Manager, but his primary duty would be forensic accounting. And after the conversion to Gyannt was complete, he would very likely take over for Melanie as the rooms division manager.

"Oh," said Demetria, looking distinctly troubled. Kurt wouldn't like this at all, just the same way he hadn't liked Melanie's sudden arrival. "I'll … see if he's in …" she said.

She walked out from behind her desk and tapped twice on the door before letting herself through and closing the door behind her.

Looks like Melanie was right about this place, he thought. He glanced across the secretary's desk, and noticed a yellow sticky-slip marked DemiFall2019. *Among other things, they need to work on password security. This will be interesting.*

Melanie Nador tried to sleep. There wasn't much else to do. She was afraid to turn on her computer, for fear that it would "phone home" or otherwise give her away. There weren't any magazines in the room, and the only book was a Bible in the top drawer of the left-hand nightstand.

Turning on the TV was out; she couldn't risk someone passing by and hearing the noise, or seeing the faint blue-white flicker from the screen reflected in the window curtains. Steve had kindly brought in food, until last night. Today, she had foraged from the mini-fridge, drinking a couple of overpriced sodas and eating a down-right expensive candy bar.

There was a knock at the door.

Melanie panicked. A thousand thoughts all went through her mind at once: Oleg had found her, and she was a dead woman. A housekeeper was coming to freshen the room; no, a contractor to fix the heater. A hired killer!

She flopped down on the floor, in the narrow space between the bed and the wall. Maybe they'd look in and not see her, and they'd go away. But…

The bed was wrinkled. They'd know she had been lying on it!

The knock was repeated.

She was tempted to dash over and peek through the peephole, but she'd seen too many movies in which doing that got the main character shot. She really did not want to be shot.

Sitting up, she tried to straighten the bedspread, to hide her presence.

"Melanie Nador!" said a deep raspy voice. "This is Sheriff Edgar Langer of the Pacific County Sheriff's department. Please open the door. We need to speak to you."

She leaped to her feet and dashed to the door. The peephole showed a very police-like man in a tan uniform. Someone else was standing behind him.

She threw open the door. "Well, it's about time."

Celia was in high dudgeon. She couldn't log into the network. She had double-checked her password, and it was right. The eyeball symbol next to the password turned the little dots into letters, and it was, letter-perfect, the password she had used every day for the past three years.

Celia said a bad word. She'd have to reset her password. That wouldn't be difficult; merely annoying. She had Marigold's login. Thanks to Oleg's foresight, Marigold, the HR manager, was a junior system administrator, and could make changes to user status.

She typed Marigold's username and the password that she had memorized for her. The computer logged her in and showed her a blotter area to work in, with all her icons. Then the screen darkened and a large box popped up, in the center of the screen:

WELCOME MARIGOLD. You are logged in on terminal tty056. Do you wish to log off of the other session?

That was strange. Marigold, as a junior system administrator, could be logged into multiple sessions at once. What did that mean?

Celia tapped the "Yes" button, and the message box went away. She swung the mouse cursor across the single screen to the Network Manager app, but the icon was gone. Network Manager had vanished. In the search box, she typed it out and hit enter.

Instead of finding and opening the program, the computer opened an internet browser and offered her links to sites for help with Network Manager. Someone had gotten into the network, changed Marigold's permissions and deleted network manager from this PC.

Marigold chose that moment to walk in the door. "Celia," she said, "The computer just kicked me out. It said that someone was logged into my account from terminal tty022, whatever that is."

Celia kept a straight face. "I'm sure it's just a glitch," she said. Glitch was a good word. For people unfamiliar with computers, it excused anything unusual. "Why don't you take a break and try it again in fifteen minutes or so?"

"I've got payrolls to process," said Marigold. "And there's the new hires, I've got to get them submitted. I don't have time for glitches." She turned and stormed out.

Too bad, thought Celia. *I need your access.*

Without Network Manager, Celia wouldn't be able to reset her password, but maybe she could do what she needed to do as Marigold. She brought up the accounting screen and clicked on the trial ledger.

It opened, showing her the last fifty actual transactions in the system. Three were batches of credit cards; the rest were checks and debits against the main account. Good, all perfectly ordinary.

Celia's fears, that someone had tampered with her accounts to keep her out of the books, appeared to be unfounded. Nonetheless, she opened the banking page and started to log in.

MARIGOLD has logged in on tty056, she read, as the screen went blank and returned to a login request.

Celia breathed a bad word and tried her own login again. It failed. Pursing her lips, she picked up the phone and dialed Oleg's extension. It rang four times and went to voicemail.

Of course he wouldn't be in his office. Why would he be? She grumbled at her bad luck and tried Kurt.

"Executive Offices," said Demetria, picking up the call from her secretarial line. "Kurt Foulard's line, Demetria speaking."

Celia rolled her eyes. "Demi, is Kurt in? This is urgent."

"He's busy," said Demi. Her voice dropped to a whisper. "He's interviewing a new Front Office manager."

"He's *what?*" asked Celia, momentarily distracted from her annoyance at the login problem.

"Right?" asked Demi. "I thought they weren't gonna fill that, you know, until…"

"Right, after Gyannt takes over." Celia frowned. "Look, don't say anything about this. It's not official yet."

"Want me to call you when he comes out?"

"No," said Celia. "I'm coming down there."

"There would have to be someone in accounting who was in on it," said Melanie. "Someone who would shift the accounts around to hide the money streams." She pointed to the CSV file on her screen, showing the names of people who had access to the hidden ledger. "The largest transactions are all done by Marigold."

"Who's Marigold?" asked O.

"The Human Resources manager. She's also theoretically in charge of accounting. She's on all the official state filings as the CFO and Controller."

"Why theoretically?"

"Because in real life, she's afraid of computers. If she logs into her own computer more than twice a month, I'd be surprised. I can't tell you how many times she's responded to a vital email a month late. It's a running joke at the home office."

"So someone logs in as her."

"Yes, and approves bank transactions, and keeps the hidden ledger. And when Gyannt takes over and does a forensic audit, she's the one left holding the bag."

"Can you tell who's really behind things?"

"Well, indirectly. You see, Marigold logs in from a lot of PCs, often at the same time. A decent security program would flag that as impossible travel. She can't be up there, on the hill, and down at the lodge within seconds."

"And these PCs all have definite physical locations, then," said Langer, nodding.

"Yes. One of them, tty022, is in the accounting office. It is most often logged into by Celia Martin. She's the assistant controller, under Marigold. But Marigold – the fake Marigold – seems to log in on that account quite often also."

"Is that a smoking gun?" asked O.

"Not quite; I don't know if it would hold up in court. Another terminal, less frequent, is tty037. It's in the Food and Beverage manager's office."

"Oleg Rustoff," said O, with a knowing nod of his head. "That ties to the wine scam."

Melanie raised her eyebrows. "Wine scam? There's a wine scam, too?"

"We'll explain later," said Langer. "Who else logs into this file as Marigold? Or, where, that is."

"Well, this one is mainly just used to check balances and download reports," said Melanie. "But tty001 is fairly active."

"And that would be?"

"Kurt Foulard."

"Never liked that guy," said Langer. "But this seems like a lot of work to hide a few bottles of wine."

"It's not about wine," said Melanie. "The main scam seems to be based on payroll. Say that I'm supposed to be making sixty-grand a year. Officially, that is."

"Is that realistic?" asked O.

"Depends on the hotel. But let's use it for round numbers. Now, in the reports to the ownership group..."

"You lost me," said Langer. "Ownership group?"

"Okay, a hotel is owned by someone. Usually it's a group of people, with different percentages of the total. Those people might be corporations, or individuals, or syndicates. Lots of ways it can work." She waved a hand dismissively. "That's the ownership group. But they don't run the hotel."

"Why not?"

"Well, usually it's because they have no experience running hotels. Sometimes it's because they want to be associated with a big name in hotel management instead of their own tiny brand. And sometimes, they're lazy. They just want to get a big check at the end of the year – a slice of the pie, so to speak."

"Okay, so who runs the hotel?"

"The management company. And they can do the books onsite, like here, or offsite, at corporate. So say I'm making sixty grand a year. Well, maybe the management group tells the ownership group that I make fifty grand a year."

"Why?" asked O. "I'd expect payroll fraud to be the other way around, claiming they pay you more, but giving you less, pocketing the difference."

"Well, that's the beauty of it," she said. "The inmates are the ones running the asylum. Foxes guarding the henhouse."

"Oh, so it comes from other streams?"

"Yes. Look at the numbers for broken crockery."

"Hmmm. That seems excessive."

"Yes, and with a bit of sketchy bookkeeping, that expense, or part of it, winds up on my paycheck. I might not even know that it's going on; it's all happening in accounting."

"Okay, so isn't it a wash? Less salary reported to the owners, more expenses reported, and either way, you get the same salary."

"Well, no. Because it gives the management group – or in this case, selected managers – the flexibility to raise or lower my salary without getting any kind of approval. And to issue bonuses. And so on. Look, to break this much crockery, this often, they'd have to be doing it deliberately."

"Amphora Hill," said O, with a smile. The others stared at him. "In ancient Rome, they imported olive oil from Spain. It was cheaper to throw the used vases overboard than to take them back for a refill. They accidentally created an artificial island in the Tiber by throwing all those clay pots into it."

"Does olive oil figure into this case somehow?" asked Langer, glaring at O. "You think Bluto's behind it all?"

"No, right, so you said, there's too much broken crockery," O said, gesturing towards the screen.

"Temporary help for events, too," said Melanie. "That is off the charts. Unless they're paying banquet waiters like doctors, this makes no sense at all."

"Fake people?"

"I'm willing to bet that there's a bank somewhere with multiple accounts each for Kurt, Oleg, and Celia. And that payroll checks for a lot of 'banquet servers' wind up being signed over into those accounts."

"Banks don't catch that?" asked Langer.

"Depends on the bank, and it depends on whether they're looking for it."

"IRS would catch it."

"Yes, if the fake employees were reported to the IRS, with proper quarterly deductions. But not if they only show up on paper, on reports to the management company, and through them to the ownership group."

"*Put not your faith in princes,*" said O. "So, what else?"

"Well, there's insurance – the hotel has about four times the normal coverage. And there are some very specific riders about fires starting in or near the kitchen."

"Fake policies?" asked Langer.

"Doesn't look like it," said Melanie. "But it's pretty fishy. And speaking of fish, this seafood budget would buy half the Alaskan salmon in the next fishing season."

O turned to Langer. "Is this enough for arrest warrants?"

"I haven't gotten to the good part," said Melanie. "There's a good four to five million extra in rooms revenue each month. We'd have to be selling every room for about three hundred extra per night, every night of the year. Always sold out, all the time.

"But it all seems to get taken up in temporary housekeeping help and damaged linen. Our cost per occupied room is an industry world record."

Langer shook his head. He looked at O. "I'd have to check with the DA." He walked over to the bedside phone. "Does this phone work?"

His radio crackled to life. "South Bend Dispatch to Sheriff Langer," came Aiden's velvet tones.

"Go for Langer," he replied.

"There is a Lieutenant Jones to see you, out of California. He's in your office."

Chapter Fifteen.

CELIA STORMED INTO THE executive offices. Demetria looked up at the extremely angry accountant and tried to hide behind her computer screen.

Reggie Pinn opened the door to Kurt's office, letting himself out as Celia pushed past him. "Kurt," she yelled, as she slammed the door. "What the hell is going on here?"

Reggie smiled at Demetria. "I can see that this will be a simply fascinating place to work."

He looked back at the closed door to the GM's office, from which Celia's voice resonated. Then he looked back at Demetria, who was staring at the door in wide-eyed horror.

"In answer to the question that you're thinking," he said. "No, warning him that she was coming would not have helped."

Reggie walked very casually out of the office.

"What are you talking about?" barked Kurt.

"Someone changed my password to the computer system. And now I can't log in as Marigold, either, because she's no longer a junior administrator. She keeps bumping me off when she logs in. Honestly, someone's been screwing around, and there's only three of us who know what to mess with."

"Are you afraid Melanie hacked Marigold's account? Don't be silly. Besides, even Gyannt would fire her for that."

"Someone did. I managed to get on long enough to check that the hidden ledgers haven't been tampered with, then Marigold bumped me off.

"I need you to log into the online banking. I can't get in, and Oleg's not in his office. I can't reach him on the phone."

"How about if I just reset your password?"

"Do not mess with me right now, Kurt. Log into the online banking system."

"Alright," he grumbled. "There, satisfied?" He spun his monitor around so that she could see it.

"That can't be right," she said. "There should be over 75 million in the transfer account."

"What is it now... fifteen thousand?" He stared at the screen. "How did that happen?"

"It's Oleg," she said. "He's a making a run."

"Louis won't like that."

Her voice dropped from shouting to a low hiss. "I don't like that either, you idiot! Neither do you! That's *our* money!"

Kurt's eyes popped wide open as the penny finally dropped. "Where's Oleg?" He threw open the door. "Demetria, get me Oleg on the phone."

"He's not on the phone," said Celia. "And he's not going to answer." She turned to Demetria. "Have the valets misplace Oleg's keys. No one leaves this island until we get some answers."

Oleg, at that moment, was between a rock and a hard place. A small panel behind the wall of the Seaside Room opened into a void. There, the inside wall of the meeting room, newly decorated with bullet holes, stood off some two and a half feet from the rough-hewn granite face behind it.

It was the only access point to the rock face. The narrow gap, sometimes relatively wide and sometimes very tight, allowed an able person to navigate slowly inside the wall, with access to the cables and pipes that supplied the hotel.

Oleg's interest lay in one pipe in particular, and one fitting. He had a pipe wrench in one hand, and as he squeezed along the wall, turning to move along the lower hallway, he worried that the clanking of the wrench would give him away.

The fitting, a union in an inch-and-a-half black iron gas pipe, lay directly under the kitchens. If the union nut were to be loosened slightly, and the union were struck with the heel of a hand, a fairly big gas leak could be produced.

Years ago, back in the planning stages, Oleg had worked this out with an engineer, sent by Louis. Once the union was opened, propane would begin to dissipate through the space beneath the kitchen floor. It would take a while to find a gap into the kitchen; the floor had been made of sturdy stuff. There was a layer of concrete, and over that a thin mortar, and then the terra cotta tiles, and then a sealant. The gas would not get through easily.

But it would get through. Drain pipes, conduits, water lines… all of these penetrated the floor, and none of them had perfect watertight seals.

Once it began to seep into the kitchen, it would take it a while to reach the sweet spot of air-fuel mixture. When almost three percent of the air in the kitchen was replaced by propane, the mixture would be flammable, and one of the pilot lights on the stoves would ignite it.

The engineer estimated that it would take about twenty-two minutes, with a small margin of error, for the explosion to happen. It would badly burn, and likely kill, most of the kitchen workers; it would send flames out into the dining room that would ignite the fabrics, carpets, seat cushions, napkins, and tablecloths.

But that would be over in a moment, with little structural damage done. The flames, at the spots where the gas penetrated the floor, however, would turn into miniature torches, keeping a steady fire burning as long as the pocket of gas beneath the floor could supply it. These jets of flame would wear down the fire-resistant sheetrock, exposing and igniting the wooden structure of the hotel.

By the time fire crews out of Long Beach managed to make their way across the narrow bridge onto the island, the main building would be fully involved; its uncontrollable inferno fueled by the propane jet under the floor. The hotel would burn, and the embers would collapse the structure on top of the computer servers and network switches. There would be no forensic examination of the servers; there would be no servers left.

Oleg struggled along the passage, sometimes stepping on his own feet in the narrow gap. Once, he banged his knee painfully on a rock outcropping.

It took him ten minutes to reach the union. He would have about twenty-two minutes to escape, from the engineer's estimate. That would leave about ten minutes, plus a small margin, to grab his briefcase and the wine crate from his office, and to get down to the treatment plant.

The engineer had said to bring two pipe wrenches, but Oleg could only find one. Besides, they were unwieldy to carry when squeezing along between the walls and the rock face. He put the pipe wrench onto the union nut, and at first it didn't seem large enough. He had to move the jaw so far out that it barely stayed connected to the threaded ring, but he managed to get it to bite on the fitting.

He pulled hard, and felt the fitting move, but the nut was still tight. He adjusted the jaw, rotating it farther back on the nut. He pulled again, this time leaning back as he tugged at it. The fitting turned, but the entire union turned, tightening itself onto the pipe at one side, and slightly loosening at the other.

That was why the engineer said to bring two wrenches, he realized. *Too late now.* He moved the wrench again and tugged again, turning the fitting a bit more. There was a squeak from the pipe to his right. He imagined that he smelled the slightest hint of propane.

Alright, he thought. *The nut isn't going to break loose, but if I can turn the fitting far enough, the threads will start to leak.* He got another grip on the big nut, and leaned back as he pulled hard with both hands. The fitting turned another few degrees before stopping.

The jaw of the wrench slipped out of the threaded ring, making the wrench come apart in his hand. The jaw skittered away in the narrow horizontal space under the floor. The ring fell straight down, into the dirt.

The aluminum handle came back at him as he fell backwards, onto the rock face. A chunk of granite rang his bell before the handle smacked into his cheekbone and nose.

He cursed, throwing the handle down into the dirt and debris at the bottom of the space. It had to be leaking by now, and if it wasn't, that was too bad. It would be too late for them to catch him, servers or no servers, once he was safely in the boat.

"Haven't seen him," said a banquet waiter, when Kurt asked him. "But I think I saw his jacket in the Seaside room."

Kurt stuck his head into the meeting room. There was a dark gray suit jacket tossed casually over a chair, but no other sign of Oleg. He grimaced and darted up to the food and beverage office.

The office door was locked. He pounded on it for a minute, then stepped into the tasting room. A server was passing through with an armload of napkins.

"Oleg?" she said, when questioned. "I think I saw him going downstairs a couple minutes ago. By your office."

Celia was having no better luck in the café and in the kitchen, areas that should have had Oleg's constant attention. She had called his cell phone six times, and tried his office phone five.

She hadn't planned for this. She had planned for a quick escape, if things went badly. She had planned for a casual escape, if things went well. But the one idea that had never crossed her mind was outright treachery, which rendered all her escape plans moot. To run now, without the money, would be to make herself an obvious suspect; a wanted fugitive with nowhere to go, no means to get there, and no money to pay off the officials when she arrived.

She stopped and stood still for a moment, and in a flash, in a blindingly clear second of epiphany, the best course of action became clear. She needed to return to her office, act like she knew nothing, and blame it all on Kurt. The key transactions were all done under Marigold's login, and it would be easy to let everyone assume that Kurt was a criminal mastermind. Well, everyone who didn't actually know him.

With a casual sigh, she let go of the tiger's tail and began to walk up the hill. Oleg had won. For now.

She would call Louis once the smoke cleared, and she would let him sort it all out. Louis knew people. He could probably have Oleg tracked down, wherever he ran to. To Louis, she would simply blame it all on Oleg.

By the time she got back into her office, she was starting to accept the direction that the day was headed.

Langer unholstered the M1911A-1 that graced his belt. He removed the magazine and then handed both to O. It was large and bulky in O's hand. "It's cocked and locked," said Langer. "You know how to use it?"

"I don't know if I can," said O, even as his left hand slid the magazine back into place.

"Just flick the safety off; that lever there by your right thumb. Then point it at the bad guy and squeeze the trigger. There's one in the chamber, and the magazine will feed the next round each time."

"It's not that I don't know how. It's that I don't know if I will be able to pull the trigger. In my mind, I mean. The last time I held a gun, three people died."

"And eighteen lived. Plus all the future bank customers they would have killed. Plus you." Langer nodded. "I have faith in you, O. When you need to, you will."

O looked at the heavy device in his hand. John Browning had a lot to answer for. But that wasn't fair; to judge the toolmaker for the use of the tool. It was O who had a lot to answer for.

"Just keep her safe. Don't let anything bad happen to her until I can get a deputy down here to take her to South Bend. You might not even have to use that thing." He shook his head. "As if I didn't have enough problems right now, I have to go deal with this Lieutenant Jones."

After Langer let himself out, O stood beside the window and moved the curtain slightly with his hand. He could see part of the path, towards the octagon building. Flakes of snow were falling again, and the path was slowly turning white. That was good; it would show the trail of anyone approaching from that way.

Oleg was slightly startled to see the sheriff's car in the circle, and the sheriff jogging down the trail from the Stone house. Oleg ignored him and wheeled the hand truck down the long, winding ramp towards ground level.

It was starting to snow again, with little flakes turning the path white. The wheels of the hand truck left a clear path through the faint dusting of snow. Oleg kept his head down and concentrated on those tire marks as he guided the crate down the ramp.

He put his hand on top of the crate, to steady his briefcase.

The sheriff, as Oleg hoped, paid no attention to the manager with the dusty pants, and instead jumped into his car, heading quickly over the bridge and out of sight.

Coincidence, he thought, calming his conscience. *There's no way they could know yet. Play it cool. Keep walking.*

His briefcase slid off of the top of the crate, landing lopsided in a bush alongside the path. A restaurant server was passing by and grabbed it for him.

"Here you go," said Rina, starting to put the briefcase back on top of the crate.

"You know," said Oleg, putting on his painful professional smile, "Why don't you carry that for me, if you don't mind? I just need to take these down there." He made a vague gesture in the general direction of the treatment plant.

She looked at the dusty face, with a growing bruise on his cheekbone and a scrape on his nose. He was wheeling a crate of wine down the path; someone should be doing that for him. And why would he want to take a crate of wine to the employee parking area, or to the wastewater treatment plant?

Something felt off about the situation. But he was one of the senior managers of the hotel, so she didn't feel comfortable questioning him. And if he was doing something wrong, it wasn't her problem. Rina ignored the little voice in her head.

"Sure," she said, following along as he wheeled the hand truck off the curb, across the circle driveway, and down towards the gravel parking area, east of the bridge.

As far as she knew, all that was down this way were the wastewater plant and some of the cottages. But she supposed that there could be a good reason to take wine to the water plant.

Reggie Pinn walked over to the tiny office he was assigned, looked quickly at its tiny utilitarian space, and then walked over to Melanie's office door.

"That's the wrong office," said Becka, looking up from a reservations call and covering the phone mouthpiece with her hand.

"It's okay," said Reggie, as he inserted his key and opened the door. Becka stared, certain that Oleg and Arne had been arguing over opening that door earlier. But duty called, and she turned her attention back to the call.

She will have left me something, he thought. *Some clue to what she's up to.* He sent his eyes around the tiny room, looking for the thing that was out of place. When nothing presented itself, he walked around behind the desk and sat down. He repeated the scan with his eyes, and at the same time sent his fingertips to the edges and unseen surfaces around him. One of his fingers felt something on the back edge of the desk, where this office shared a wall with his office.

It was a bump; a bit of tape over a small hard object, about the size of his little fingernail. He smiled. Good old Melanie. It would be a micro-SD chip, and the data he needed would all be there.

Kurt found himself in an uncomfortable position. It was caused in part by the muzzle of the gun that dug into his ribs. It was exacerbated by the South Asian man walking closely behind him, who was holding that pistol. Kurt was accustomed to being obeyed; to giving orders and having them followed without question, so to have this man march him down the path of his own hotel was intolerably uncomfortable. It was simply undignified.

"What's your game plan?" asked Kurt, in hopes of dissuading the man from killing him. "Take me out to the woods and shoot me? Then, what? Have you thought this through?"

"Shut up," said the small, thin South Asian man.

"There are people staying in all the cabins. They'll see you. They'll hear you. Listen, we can work this out."

The gun dug deeper into his ribs. "I'm telling you to shut up."

The gentle snow continued to fall. The sparse flakes melted immediately on touching the men's clothing, but the path was taking a pale hue, and the greenery alongside the path was glistening with dampness. In a few minutes, it would surrender and become part of a thin white sheet.

Kurt had a vision of his blood staining that white sheet. Of Langer standing over him, shaking his head, unable to solve the crime. Of the hotel, weeping for their lost leader.

The South Asian nudged him.

"What's your name?" asked Kurt. He had once read that hostages should humanize themselves. Also, having a name would give him a handle to use, a means to normalize this odd turn of events. He could speak to this man in the proper tone, and make him feel his place, at which point he would surely see that pointing a gun into Kurt's ribs was simply not the way to do things.

"It is not something which matters," said the man.

Kurt stopped and turned towards him.

"I am called Sandip, if you must know," said the man, with a sigh. "Now you will start walking or I will shoot you. First in the foot, but not too badly. Because I will need for you to be walking. Which you are going to do, right now." The gun dug into Kurt's side, so he started walking.

"Sandip, Listen, I can help you," said Kurt.

"Already you have been bungling this operation until I have had to be sent here. It is a shambles. Do not be telling me what you can help. If you do not do as I say, I will be putting bullets into you and then Louis can figure out what to do with the hotel. Clear?"

"Very clear," said Kurt, realizing at last that his world was caving in. This man was not some random felon. He was a stone-cold killer, and had been sent by Louis, to kill Kurt and to mop things up. No wonder Oleg had run. But Oleg should have told Kurt and Celia, shouldn't he? It was maddening, that Oleg would have so little respect.

Louis on the one side, Langer on the other, and Oleg running away just when Kurt needed him most. Kurt was livid. People were not supposed to treat him like this.

"When we first reach the cabin, you will knock at the door," said Sandip. "I will be saying nothing. She will open the door for you, then I will shoot her, and you can go your way."

Sandip had no intention of letting Kurt go his own way. In fact, he would try very hard to make it look as if Kurt had killed Melanie, and then killed himself. It wouldn't make a lot of sense to the police, but Sandip had seen it done like that on television, and was certain that it would work.

Kurt also realized that he was, for the moment, a walking dead man. It was clear, even to him, that no matter what happened at the cabin, he had almost no chance of walking away. Unfortunately for him, he lacked imagination, and so he saw no alternative but to follow Sandip's plan.

O's system of glancing out the windows every few minutes, first to one side of the door and then to the other, finally paid off. Two men were walking down the path towards them, coming from the main lodge side. The one in front seemed reluctant, and the one walking too close behind him seemed to be nudging him to keep him moving.

With the faint snowfall dampening the glass and obscuring the view, it took O a moment to realize that the man in front was Kurt Foulard, the General Manager. From the awkward way that they moved, the second man, a thin dark man with South Asian features, must have held a gun on Kurt.

He snapped his fingers twice. Melanie looked up from the laptop, her fingers hovering above the keys.

"Go into the bathroom and lock the door. Lie down inside the shower stall. Cover yourself with a towel. Move now."

"Why the shower?" she asked, as she got up, closing the laptop and taking it with her..

"The tiles won't stop bullets," he said. "But they may help to attenuate them. You won't be hurt as badly. And throw towels over yourself for the fragments. Do it now."

Frightened, she did as he said. He heard the door click behind him, and then the shower glass sliding. He hoped it was tempered glass, for her sake.

He looked down at the gun in his hand. It was a big gun, a traditional war piece, a relic of the second great war. It felt solid and dependable in his hand. It fired .45 caliber bullets, capable of knocking a man down, if they hit him properly. The bullets wouldn't penetrate deeply into wood, so shooting through the solid wooden door would leave almost no energy in the bullet to injure the assassin.

Shooting through the glass, on the other hand, might inspire the assassin to simply stick his hand through the window and fire randomly into the room. Or, worse yet, to lob in a grenade, if he had one. It was best not to draw attention to the vulnerable windows, at least for now.

It was unlikely that the assassin would have a grenade, but O couldn't take the chance. He really didn't yet know who he was up against. Or how many; there might be backup hiding nearby.

What were his options? Yank open the door and shoot first? Wait and open the door slowly, gun hidden, playing a cool hand? Let himself be disarmed … no, that never ended well.

The pair was approaching the door. It was a left hand door, and the South Asian man was behind Kurt and slightly to his right.

A plan formed in his mind. If he played it well, it might work… provided Kurt could be gotten out of the way fast enough.

156

O took the chain off of the door, allowing it to dangle beside the doorjamb. He crouched to the right of the doorway, gun in his right hand, doorknob in his left.

As Kurt knocked, O pulled the door open a few inches. Sandip's hand darted up, squeezing off a shot where O's head would be if he were standing. At the sudden snap-pop of Sandip's .22, Kurt threw himself face down in the snow.

O fired once, a snap shot, without aim. The .45 roared, startling Sandip, who was suddenly completely unshielded.

Melanie was supposed to be unarmed. The noise of the old war-piece made him jump back, smacking his head on the rustic iron porch lamp suspended by the door.. His feet slipped, and he almost fell down.

O fired again, still not really aiming, this time grazing Sandip's coat. He quickly pulled the door closed and swung himself to his left, behind the door, as Sandip fired a volley of .22 rounds, aimed where O had been. The shots embedded themselves in the door and the doorjamb.

He stopped shooting when the pistol was empty. O looked out the window, seeing Sandip jerking the trigger of the unresponsive gun. He shattered the glass with the muzzle of the 1911, just as Sandip realized that his gun was empty and dropped the magazine into the snow.

O put one quick shot out the window, again without aiming. He saw a chunk of bark fly off of a pine tree, behind Sandip.

Sandip, realizing that his position was indefensible, ducked behind another large tree, and using it to shield him from the cabin window, backed away from the cabin.

O had no clear shot at him from the window. When he was far enough away, Sandip turned and ran back through the trees, trampling the flowerbeds.

O spun back to right and opened the door for a better shot. Kurt, who had been lying in the snow the entire time, leaped to his feet, saw the gun in O's hand, and followed Sandip's example by running blindly down the path. With Kurt in the way, O didn't have any clear shot.

"Stay there!" shouted O, to Melanie, as he slammed the door behind him and ran after Sandip.

O did not have a clear plan. What would he do when he caught him? Shoot him in the back, in cold blood? Tackle him, like a football player, and possibly allow Sandip to shoot him with the reloaded twenty-two? Or would he just dart down into the circle, waving a gun in the air, like the murderous madman that the hotel staff already thought he was?

He stopped behind a large eucalyptus, slid the gun into his pants pocket, and walked quickly down the path. Snowflakes, melting on his forehead, made his hair start to stick to his brow.

As he reached the loading dock, he caught a glimpse of Sandip, who had turned his small head start into a big lead, and was already running over the bridge. *Fouled out of play*, he thought. *Even if I caught him, I couldn't reliably subdue him.*

At that moment, a small Mercedes-Benz E-Class backed past him out of the loading dock, whipping around in a semicircle, and sliding slightly on the slick pavement. It stopped as the rear bumper nudged a low stone wall. Wheels spinning, it shifted to a forward gear and shot around the circle, towards the bridge.

Foulard, thought O. *No point in running after him.* He stood for a moment, assessing the situation, then started to turn back toward the Stone House.

Motion on the bridge caught his eye. Foulard's Mercedes spun sideways on the slick surface, stopping itself between the concrete rails. O watched for a moment as Kurt tried in vain to go forward or backwards, but the few inches of space on each end of the car did not give enough room for Kurt to maneuver, even if Kurt had had the skills or the nerve to free the stuck car.

O shook his head and started to run towards the Stone House, when he spotted Rina in the employee parking area, struggling with a hand truck. Oleg was standing with her. Oleg was obviously making his own escape, this one slightly more subtle than Kurt's. And that escape clearly involved Rina. O couldn't allow that. He couldn't let innocent people get hurt by the hornet's nest that he had stirred up.

O ran cautiously towards them, His right hand wrapped around the M1911 in his pants pocket.

Oleg and Rina appeared to be trying to move a crate of wine on a hand truck, but the gravel in the lot and the steady snowfall were making it difficult. The wheels of the hand truck, tiny plastic disks made for hard sidewalks, were catching and dragging in the gravel, plowing it up in front of them.

As O drew near, Oleg looked up from the hand truck. He raised a pistol and shot at O, missing both times.

O returned fire, carefully putting two rounds into the tire of a parked car. He slowed from a trot to a brisk walk, gun pointed at Oleg's head. His arms naturally moved into a two-handed thumbs-parallel grip, elbows slightly bent, left hand supporting the right.

Oleg grabbed Rina around the shoulders and pointed his gun to her temple. It was smaller than the gun Langer had lent O. It looked like a Beretta 92S, in 9 millimeter. Rina still held the small black briefcase, but she had raised it in front of her chest, like a shield. O knew that it wouldn't be effective at stopping bullets. He had to make sure that he only hit his target.

Could he hit Oleg's head at this range? Probably. Could he be absolutely certain the shot wouldn't go low and right, into Rina's head? Not absolutely. He held his fire.

Oleg was whispering something into her ear as they backed towards the wastewater plant. For each step O took forward, Oleg took one backward. O didn't stop.

"Who sent you?" asked Oleg. "Are you Lou's man?"

"I'm just a guy," said O. "A guy holding a gun on you."

"I'll shoot her."

"Let's see how that goes: You shoot her, she falls down, no reason for me not to put three bullets into your chest." O shook his head slowly, never taking his eyes off Oleg. "You won't do that."

Oleg glanced over his shoulder, making sure he was lining up with the gateway into the plant.

"You just walk away, okay? Forget about all this." he said. "I'll wire you some money. Lots of money. I'll make you rich. Name your number."

"Even if I trusted you, I couldn't do that."

"There's money in the briefcase," said Oleg. "Drop it, Rina, let him have it."

Rina reluctantly lowered and then slowly let go of the briefcase. It fell beside her, and then fell over. It lay there, a black rectangle in the white lot, as Oleg and Rina backed away from it. Her arms fluttered; without her shield, she didn't know whether to put her arms in front of her chest or down at her sides.

"Look inside," shouted Oleg.

O knew that if he tried to touch the briefcase, Oleg would have a clear shot at the top of his head. Only the fact that his gun was pointed at Oleg's face was keeping him alive. Mutually assured destruction.

He ignored the briefcase and kept walking towards the pair.

"Rina, fall down," said O.

She went limp, collapsing at Oleg's feet. It caught Oleg off-guard, and he started to bend forward as she fell, then realized what was happening and pointed his gun at O.

Oleg and O fired at the same time. O's shot caught Oleg in the sternum, and the man dropped face down in the snow next to Rina. Rina jumped up and ran to O, hiding behind him as she peered back at Oleg. Then she darted for the main lodge, her feet crunching the gravel.

O kept the gun on Oleg as the sound of Rina's steps faded. He kicked out, using his toe to straighten Oleg's arms until he could see the gun. With a couple more careful kicks, he knocked it well away from Oleg before squatting to pick it up.

Putting a knee on Oleg's back, he reached down with his left hand and checked for a carotid pulse. There wasn't one. He tucked the .45 into his belt, behind his back, and then rolled Oleg over.

CPR wouldn't help. The bullet was clearly fatal, the wound channel leading directly to Oleg's heart. There was no point in compressions; the heart still wasn't going to pump blood.

O stood up straight and walked back the way he had come, towards the lodge. It was time to call in Langer.

As he neared the bridge, he saw the flashing lights of Langer's car on the other side, near Dead Man's Cove. On closer inspection, it appeared that the doors were standing open.

Kurt's Mercedes was still in the middle of the bridge, and the driver's door was open on it as well. He imagined that Langer was chasing down Kurt in the snowy woods of Cape Disappointment.

He thought about going over to help, but it was probably too late. Instead, he walked back to the Stone house.

Kurt ran down the sloping bridge, towards Dead Man's Cove. There was only one road off the island; the narrow spit of highway that led up into Ilwaco, so his options for escape were limited. He found himself slipping and sliding on the slick pavement of the bridge, waving his hands around in the air like an orchestra conductor on LSD.

It didn't matter. Dignity, for once, didn't matter. Nothing mattered but getting as far from the hotel as possible. He shouldn't be the one fleeing for his life; it was patently unfair that the universe should expect this of him. Still, he ran. It was all he could do.

As he reached ground level, he saw the flashing lights peeking through the trees, reflecting off of the falling snowflakes, and sending odd red and blue beams across the field, like a madman's lighthouse. Any second now, the police car radiating those lights would come around the corner, and he'd have nowhere left to run.

Over the rail he went, sliding down the berm into a grassy field. The grasses were now covered in a thin coating of white, but they were there. Every step he took sent his feet through the white layer into the shin-deep damp grasses below. His socks were soaked through already; his expensive shoes were ruined. He was certain that the legs of his slacks would never be the same.

A trail of footprints led away at a different angle, reaching from the road to the thick stand of trees, and for a moment he was tempted to follow them. Where there was another person, there would be someone whom he might convince of his superiority; someone upon whom he might impose to escape this madness.

But the goal was to escape; to be where no one could find him. If someone knew where he was, he might be betrayed. For once, he was better off alone. So he continued his run, straight for the tree line.

He had almost reached the safety of the forest when the flashing lights came past the tree line. He looked over his shoulder and tripped, falling face first into the wet grasses. Jumping to his feet, he scrambled into the forest, and stood breathlessly staring from behind a tree, as the first car, Ilwaco police, shot up the bridge and then slid to a sudden stop. He cringed, expecting to hear the car slam into his Mercedes. But it did not.

The second car, with a Pacific County logo on the door, pivoted off the road and bounced through the grassy field, cutting a swatch through the blanket of white. They had seen his trail. They were coming for him. They were almost on him.

He turned into the forest and tried to run, but he was exhausted. His legs refused to work, and he went down in a pile of snow and pine needles. Hands grabbed his arms, and then he was moving back to the Sheriff's car.

"Kurt Foulard," said Sheriff Langer. "I am arresting you as a material witness in the murder of Jackson Johns."

Kurt looked up, as they cuffed him, staring into the forest, to where his dreams were escaping. Sandip stepped out from behind a tree and laid the silencer of his pistol across his lips, as if to shush him. Then Sandip was gone from sight.

Chapter Sixteen

"IT WAS ALL OLEG. Get him in here, he'll tell you."

"We can't do that, Mr. Foulard," said the deputy. "Now, would you be so kind as to initial the form in front of you and to indicate whether you do or do not wish to speak with an attorney at this time?"

Kurt scribbled on the paper and thrust it towards the deputy.

"It was Oleg," he said. "Jackson called us up to the cupola room, the one at the top of the stairs. It seemed important. Ask him. Oleg, I mean."

"We can't do that, Mr. Foulard."

"You haven't found him?" Kurt made it sound as if he were gravely disappointed, and would bring this up at the deputy's next performance review.

"Oh, we know right where he is, Sir." The deputy smiled. "Are you comfortable? Sheriff Langer will be here in a minute, once he finishes with what he's doing."

Kurt's nostrils flared at the idea that the sheriff could be doing something more important than talking to him.

"Look, you may not know who I am." Kurt raised his head and tried to look dignified, in spite of the fact that his hands were cuffed to a metal ring on the table.. "The sheriff and I are old friends. I helped him solve the last murders, a few years ago."

The deputy smiled again. "I'll be sure to let him know that."

"Can't we just settle this right now?" asked Kurt. "Get Oleg Rustoff on here. He'll tell you that I'm innocent. I never touched Jackson Johns."

"That's not going to happen."

"And just why not?"

"He's dead."

Kurt stopped and floundered for a moment, wide-eyed, as he assimilated this new information. "Well, I didn't do that."

"No, Sir. Deputy Johnson shot him."

Kurt had no idea who Deputy Johnson was, but he decided to send the man a Christmas card. Maybe he'd include one of his business cards, with a personal note on the back.

"Well, that's too bad," he said, settling back slightly in the chair. "We met with Jackson at the top of the stairs, in the little room there. He had wine bottles up there to show us. Apparently he wanted to make sure we weren't overheard."

"Nice of him," said the deputy. "You didn't want to wait for the sheriff, or maybe your lawyer?"

"Lawyers," said Kurt. "Who needs them? We can clear this up right now, can't we?"

The deputy shrugged. "Up to you," he said.

"He was a nice man," said Kurt. "But a bit of a drunk. So, anyway, he started ranting, accusing us of some sort of nefarious plot. He said we had to stop selling wine until we settled it.

"It was insane stuff. We make our money on food and wine. But he wouldn't settle down. Fake wines. Fake bottles. Reselling the same wine, over and over. I told him he was crazy and walked out, but Oleg stayed to try to talk him down."

"Makes sense," said the deputy.

"Well, as Oleg told it to me later, Jackson thought Oleg was attacking him. He pulled a kitchen knife on him. Oleg tried to take it away, you know, for his own safety, and apparently Jackson backed out onto the roof.

"Oleg didn't want him to fall off, you know, being drunk as he was and holding a knife like that. So he went out after him."

"And to keep him safe, he stabbed him and threw him off the roof," said the deputy. "Makes perfect sense to me."

"You're being sarcastic."

"Maybe a little."

Kurt gave him another stern look. "Oleg had only the best intentions. But Johns was drunk; what else could he do?"

"Well, he could do like you said that you did," said the deputy. "If Johns really was crazy, all he had to do was walk away."

"Yes, but ..." said Kurt. Words failed him, so he relied instead on his look of superiority, as if he simply had no words to express how foolish the deputy sounded.

"And it hardly matters. You both took part in a felony that resulted in a death. You're as guilty as he is." The deputy shrugged.

"It's not a felony to try to calm a man who is raving about some insane plot."

"No, but it's a felony to defraud your customers, and to try to silence a witness."

"Are you sure that how it works?"

"Pretty sure. But the DA will be able to sort it all out." The deputy shrugged. "He should be along soon. After the sheriff comes by for a few questions, you know."

Kurt sat still. Murder? That was simply silly. He didn't murder anyone. Johns just fell off the roof, after Oleg stabbed him.

"Honestly," said Celia, as she sat at the tiny table in the little room at the Sheriff's station, "I have no idea why I'm here."

"No idea at all," said O, with a smile, watching her through the one-way glass. "It couldn't be five years of laundering money and defrauding the hotel owners."

Sheriff Langer slid a paper in front of her. "Well, we just need to clear up a few things, then we can send you on your way," he said. "This paper acknowledges that we talked about your right to an attorney, if you would just sign there... Excellent, and now if you'll initial that you're waiving an attorney, good. There we go."

He slipped the acknowledgement into a manila folder that lay in front of him. With the return of his hand, he drew out a slip of paper. "Is that your signature?"

Celia blanched slightly, but recovered well. "I've never seen that before in my life," she said.

"Odd," said Langer. "Because the accounts manager at the local bank says that you signed that paper. He identified your photograph. He says that that's your signature card for this bank account." Another paper from the folder.

"I, well." She said, and it sounded hollow, even in her own mind. She could make up ad hoc explanations for a while, but in the end, they'd trap her. Langer would pull some rabbit out of his hat, some paper from that Manila folder, and prove that she was part and parcel of the plan. It would all spill now.

There was only one way to get out of it. "Kurt made me do it," she blurted. "Kurt and Oleg, they said they needed me to run the accounting side of it, and they said they'd kill me if I told anyone. So I had to."

"Kurt and Oleg can't hurt you now," said Langer. "One's in custody, and the other's dead."

For a moment, she wondered which was which. She could imagine a confrontation between them, in which Oleg stabbed Kurt. Or she could imagine Kurt shooting Oleg. It would be best to be very non-committal, and not blame either one directly until she knew who was dead.

"We have Melanie Nador. We have the memos, the accounts, and the true ledgers. We know all about the secret money, and where it went. What we need to know is where the money came from."

Celia's eyes widened. That would be a problem. She could point to Kurt or to Oleg; they were both toothless, and could do nothing to hurt her. But Louis? No one in her right mind would cross Louis. Not unless she were very well-protected.

"I want a deal," she said. O smiled and let himself out of the observation room. Aiden was waiting in the hall.

"Well, the hero returns," she said.

"I just did–"

"What anyone would have done, that's what the hero always says. That's the way it always is." She smiled, and then she lowered her voice and gave a serious look. "You doing okay with it?"

"With shooting Oleg? Well, it's … different, I guess."

She led him to the break room and sat him at a table while she drew a cup of coffee from the coffeemaker for him. "In what way is it different?"

"I had time. I could think. I could see the possibilities, and how he was going to shoot me, or shoot Rina, or both. That's why he had her help him; he wanted a hostage. And that wouldn't have ended well. If she got onto that boat with him –"

"There was a boat?"

"Small fishing boat, with an outboard motor. They kept it at the plant for checking the outfall pipe. Apparently he was going to use it to get upriver and bum a ride on an outgoing ship."

"And take Rina with him?"

"No, once he got the boat into the river, she'd be dead weight. So she'd be dead. She was just there to be a hostage, not to actually help him move the crate."

"Did he say that?"

"No, but isn't it obvious? I mean, he's escaping; if he'd known the hand-truck wouldn't work well on the gravel, he'd have used someone else. One of the valets, right?"

"Impeccable logic," she said.

"And the other way it was different, is that I was certain about everything this time. The moral landscape, I mean. I didn't have to ask if he was a good guy or a bad guy. There was no doubt."

"The three at the bank were bad guys too."

"You know about that?"

"I made Langer tell me."

"Ah. Then you understand."

"But they were killers. You should have felt no remorse at all over that." She patted his hand. "You were a hero there, too."

"But there, I didn't think."

"You did think. You used your limbic brain, and it told you that you had to fight. So you did, and very well."

"But—"

"But your frontal lobe says you should have made sure. It always does that. Still, what your limbic brain said was right."

"I guess we'll see how I sleep."

"Like a baby, I'll bet. Hey, are you gonna need help cleaning out your place in Ilwaco?"

"Nah, I don't have much stuff there."

"Oh," she said. "Because if you need a truck, I know a guy."

"I appreciate the offer. And I appreciate the advice the other day. About controlling the dream, and releasing my brain."

"It just seemed like common sense," she said.

Langer walked in and pointed to O "You and me need some coffee." He nodded towards the door. "If you'll excuse us, Aiden."

Triple-A smiled sweetly and waved goodbye as they walked out of the room.

The waitress at the diner smiled fondly at O. Apparently she approved of his lack of sleep deprivation. She motioned them to a booth and flipped over a pair of coffee cups.

"Well, I'm glad to be done with that," said Langer, nodding when the cup was full enough.

"I assume Celia's singing."

"Like a prima donna in the spotlight. Took a little pressure, but she won't stop talking."

"And Foulard?"

"He didn't even need pressure. That man couldn't stop talking if you duct-taped his mouth shut. Also, we're trying to get out-of-state warrants on one Leon Rothenberg. Apparently he started the bookkeeping scam, but he bailed out a couple of years ago, when we were down there at the hotel, investigating some other murders. It's a long story."

"I might have heard rumors around the hotel. Somebody shot in the Stone house, and a poisoning at a mushroom luncheon."

"Something like that. Anyway, it looks like we were near enough to make him bail out."

"They probably could have milked that scam right up till the Gyannt takeover, if they hadn't started the wine scam."

"Kurt and Celia both say that was Oleg's idea. A little extra cash on top as a going-away present."

A man in a suit detached himself the counter and wandered down to them. He resembled Langer in some ways. They could have gone to the same barber, and the newcomer's mustache was the image of Langer's.

"The coffee here is nice," he said, as he spun a chair around and seated himself at the end of the table. "But I have a flight out of Portland tomorrow."

O and Langer looked him in the eye. "Do I know you?" asked Langer, with an ominous undertone in his voice.

"Not yet. Lieutenant Jones, of the Salinas Police. I came up about the gun that shot out your windows."

"Ah, sorry, Lieutenant. We got a little busy. We were wrapping up a murder case. Sorry to leave you hanging."

"Well, the dispatcher was kind enough to keep me up to date. She let me know that you'd had to turn around and go back to ... was it called Ilwaco?"

"It rhymes with taco," said O. "Not like the city in Texas."

"This is one of my officers, O Johnson. He was working there undercover," said Langer.

"O?" asked Jones.

"Like the Japanese first baseman, Sadaharu Oh," said O. "But it's my first name, and without the 'h.' "

"Ah," said Jones. The waitress, seeing that Jones' presence was being tolerated, and that he wasn't being sent back to the minors, appeared with another coffee cup and a bowl of creamers.

"Sorry you had to come all this way for nothing," said Langer. "And I still owe you for lending me your detectives a couple years ago. They came in handy."

"Yorga and Bentley had nothing but good things to say," said Jones. "But what I'd like to know about is the shooter that got away; the one that tried to clean things up his own way. We think he's part of an organized criminal group."

"Kurt and Celia are insisting that it was all Oleg Rustoff and Leon Rothenberg who masterminded everything," said Langer.

"That doesn't explain the South Asian shooter," said Jones.

"Sandip," said Langer. "No last name known. Indian – that is, South Asian – and not a particularly good shot with a pistol. In three tries, his best score was winging a night manager."

"I could work with a police artist and maybe give you a good sketch," said O. "But none of his features were really particularly unusual." O shrugged.

"I'd like the bullets you got from the crime scenes, if I can," said Jones. "And any recovered casings, or other items that may turn up. I think they link to something going on down my way."

"I'll have the lab send them once we've cataloged them and run them through NCIC. And I'll email our files down to you."

"Not through email," said Jones. "There's a reason I came up here in person. Any chance I could get you to send a courier? I'll make sure that he's set up in a nice hotel on the peninsula."

"You've got a mole?" asked O.

"Let's just say that I have reason to be concerned."

"O could use some time away from his dishwasher," said Langer. "And he's the most discreet person I know."

"I'll consider it a personal favor."

"No, it just makes us even," said Langer. He looked at Jones' untouched coffee cup. "Something wrong with the coffee?"

"No, but I think I've had my fill." He took out his business card and wrote something on the back. "When you're ready to send the courier, contact me at this number only, and do not leave a message," he said pointing to the back of the card. He rose to his feet and returned the chair to the table from which he had borrowed it.

"Nice to meet you," said O.

"And you," said Jones, as he turned towards the register. He paused and nodded to Langer. "Sheriff."

"So what's going to happen to Foulard?" asked O, when Jones was gone.

"Felony murder," said Langer. "He took part in a conspiracy, and someone died as a result. Life, most likely. Same for Celia. She may not have pulled any triggers, but she sure pulled some strings."

"You think Melanie's testimony is gonna be enough to slam the door on them?"

"Well, between that and the doctored books, I think the State of Washington will be cooking their meals for decades to come. And if they ever breathe free air, the IRS will want to talk to them about reported income."

"What's gonna come out of the thing with Oleg?"

"That's what you call it? The thing with Oleg? You stare down a cold-blooded killer, rescue his hostage, put a bullet through his pump – Justified, mind you – and you call it 'the thing with Oleg.' You have no sense of the dramatic, O."

O shrugged. He had no idea what Langer was getting at, so he let it pass. "So what happens now?"

Langer sipped his coffee. "Now we give you a medal and a parade. What do you expect?"

"The DA won't have any questions?"

"Pfft. You handed him two open-and-shut slam-dunk cases, both very high profile, and you think he's going after you for this? You shot a fleeing felon who had a hostage, O. And you were acting as a deputy. There's no case."

"Not exactly a deputy. I wasn't a sworn officer."

"Close enough." Langer waved his hand dismissively. "But how are you dealing with it?"

"Surprisingly well," said O. "It's ... to be honest, I don't know if it's something that Aiden said to me, yesterday morning, here in this diner, or if it's the fact that this time, I thought it through. Either way, I feel good about what happened."

"Don't ever tell people that you feel good about shooting someone. Trust me, that never ends well."

"He had Rina. If he had gotten her into the plant, he would have gotten her onto the boat. Once he was clear of the island, he'd have shot her. It's the only way it could play for him. So I was morally obligated to stop him, and that meant shooting him."

"Okay, but let's talk about it again in a few weeks." Langer sipped some more coffee. "Just to make sure you're still hanging together. You're still dealing with that bank thing, and that's been months now."

"Nearly a year, maybe a little more," said O. "And I'll tell you, I think I have a handle on that, too. It's like this thing somehow redeemed that thing, that shooting. Does that sound silly?"

"Not at all. I'd say it just gave you more perspective on it."

The two sat in silence for a moment, then Langer spoke up.

"The hotel's gonna lose its liquor license. Too much violence related to the sale of alcohol on the premises." Langer snickered. "Usually when this happens, it's because of drunks starting fights. Not managers throwing people off rooftops."

O grinned. "Think that's gonna ruin the deal with Gyannt hotels? I mean, no liquor, there goes the restaurant."

"They'll take a big hit on it, that's for sure. But they own the place, so what are they gonna do?"

"Maybe sell it off cheaply. Bad press and all."

"It'll all be tied up in litigation for ages. Owners sue the managers, management company sues Kurt and Celia, insurance sues everybody. Honestly, I'd expect the hotel to be closed for three or four years until the smoke settles."

"Maybe, maybe not," said O. "How's Rina?"

"Fine as frog's hair. She's not moving back in with Diane, if that's what you're wondering. I did tell her that it would be good of her to call her mother, but she's an adult, and she can do what she wants. And I gave her a pep talk; told her she did good helping to catch Oleg like that."

"Well, that's putting a good face on it. Maybe she won't have nightmares about being a hostage."

"I didn't tell her that she was a hero. Just said she handled it well, and that if I was her papa, I'd be proud of her."

"Never hurts to boost someone a bit, I guess." O sipped his coffee. "You feeling hungry, or do you suppose we should eventually get back to the office?"

Langer glanced at the refrigerated case behind the counter. "Well, I'm thinking that a slice of apple pie would go good right now. Whaddya say?"

Months later, O sat in a glass and aluminum lounge, looking out at the waves. The lounge was three stories above the beach, and the view was breathtaking. The waves seemed so close that he almost felt like pulling in his feet to keep them dry.

He shook his head at the thought. Outside, the sky was overcast, the wind was brisk, and the air was crisp. Here, in this nice heated lounge, with a cup of coffee at his elbow; here, he could sit all afternoon. He smiled to himself, savoring the stillness, as if time had stopped.

He looked up as Aiden floated into the room. She took a divan near his chair and they grinned at each other.

"You're mighty relaxed," she said, at last. "I didn't know you had it in you to unwind like this."

"I feel like the world has been lifted off of my shoulders. It may not last, but right now, right here, I am content."

She didn't say a thing, but patted his arm.

"Lieutenant Jones just left," he said, after a moment. "He picked up the papers, and then it really sounded like he was trying to recruit me for some sort of undercover skullduggery."

"Scullery to skullduggery. You're coming up in the world."

"I declined. What are we doing for dinner?"

"That one steakhouse on Cannery Row," she said. "But we've got a couple hours before we need to get ready."

"Want to sit and watch the waves for a while?"

"Nothing I'd rather do," said Aiden.

www.ingramcontent.com/pod-product-compliance
Lightning Source LLC
Chambersburg PA
CBHW030342180626
46812CB00007B/2724

* 9 7 8 1 9 4 9 0 0 5 1 8 9 *